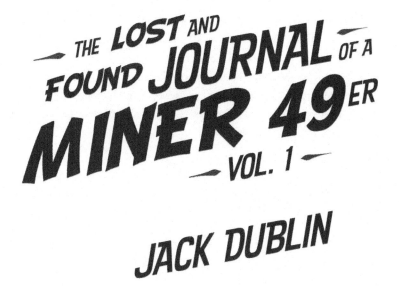

THE LOST AND FOUND JOURNAL OF A MINER 49ER VOL. 1

JACK DUBLIN

Trade Paperback Edition ISBN: 978-1-54391-725-3

eBook ISBN: 978-1-54391-726-0

Cover and interior illustrations by Tithi Luadthong

Printed in these United States of America

OLDENWORLD BOOKS

www.JackDublin.net

To the Tribes of Abigail, Ava, Troy, and Zoë...

Up the Adventure!

CONTENTS

FOREWORD

◆—◆

I n the summer of 2013, my family and I traveled to the Grand Canyon for a week of whitewater rafting down the Colorado River. When a monsoon rolled in, forcing us to higher ground, we sheltered in a cave unseen for nearly 150 years. What we found inside—several journals from the time of the California Gold Rush—contradicted the accepted version of history taught in classrooms today. To say that mankind has been bamboozled for generations would be an understatement, but that is exactly what the journals prove. My chief aim in publishing this first book of journal entries, therefore, is to set in motion the wheels of change that will carry mankind along the road of discovery to a forgotten past. In years to come, it is easy to imagine *The Lost and Found Journal of a Miner 49er* serving as a history primer, of sorts, for school children the world over.

Historical Criticism

Having established how I came in possession of the journals, the following pages will serve to demonstrate that the author was none other than the Miner 49er from the American folk song *Oh, My Darling, Clementine*; and furthermore, that the Miner 49er, whose Christian name was Cody Kirschenbaum, was not a fictional character, but a flesh-and-bone man who once walked dusty, forsaken stretches of this world, braved seas sailed by mariners of old, faced down giants with the certitude of King David, and served as an integral cog in the cultivation of the American Southwest from a wasteland into the palm tree and golf course dotted *megaloasis* (to coin a term) we find today.

If you doubt the veracity of my statement, allow me to return to that cave in the Grand Canyon as supporting evidence. The cave contained the skeletal remains of a donkey believed to be those of the longtime companion of Kirschenbaum, who answered to the name of Clip-clop; a saddlebag of journal manuscripts, or tomes, written by a single hand; a few gold and silver pieces dating to the Gold Rush era; and a curious stone about the size of a biscuit, with a purple crystal at its center—weighing an unfathomable 44.4 pounds—that has been shipped to a laboratory in the United Kingdom for further analysis. Such relics did not spring into existence from the ether but belonged to an historical figure who fits the profile of the Miner 49er.

Archaeological Criticism

Archaeologists have not recovered the bones of the Miner 49er in the four years since the original discovery of the cave. Further efforts have met with stiff resistance from the local Havasupai tribe due to an unfortunate, somewhat tawdry event involving members of a local university's archaeology department. I will not discuss the details in full here, other than the incident included flamboyant headdresses, dime-store beauty supplies and a Chinese water dragon. It is hoped that, in time, all wounds will be healed—indeed, that we shall have a good laugh about the matter—and the Havasupai people will allow further investigation into this most astonishing and important historical discovery.

So, what of it, you say? What is the 21st Century man on the street to make of these discoveries? Is it possible that the Miner 49er was an historical figure? My purpose in publishing this first installment of Kirschenbaum's journals is not to indoctrinate you into one belief or another; rather, I ask you to make up your own mind by keeping an open mind.

I will appeal to your sense of logic, with such facts as the handwritten note included in the pages of the journal from Jacob "Bubby" Waltz, Jr to "Mr. Kirschenbaum" that expresses his condolences and deep sadness at the drowning of a girl named Clementine, and a doleful plea that her death not be held to his—that is, Bubby's—account, given the fact that he was "not gifted in the water arts as you yourself [Mr. Kirschenbaum] are, but a landlubber through and through, to my own eternal shame." Might it be mere coincidence that Kirschenbaum had a daughter named Clementine who drowned, and yet she is not the same girl of whom we sing while roasting marshmallows around the campfire? I suppose—but the explanation is entirely inadequate, given the astronomical odds calculated against it.

Literary Criticism

Critics argue I should have included the journal entry *Lost and Gone Forever*, which details the events that led to the drowning of Clementine, in this book. Indeed, I have received many letters from school children around the world—too many to count—urging me to do just that. However, the time was not right. Too many readers would race past other important entries to get to that one but doing so would leave them bewildered. About this matter, I will say nothing further, other than to ask the reader to trust my judgment, seeing how the journal entries in this book were carefully selected to buttress the backstory of *Lost and Gone Forever*. When it finally is published, everyone will understand my reasons for waiting.

Contrary to rumors on the Internet, the number of journals discovered in the Miner 49er's saddlebag was not thirty-three, but seven. In addition to the seven journals, the trove included a collection of papers rolled up and knotted together by a loose leather strap. Some have called this the *Eighth Journal*, but I hesitate to call it that, since many second-hand treasure maps, astronomical charts, and open-pit baking recipes are included among the papers.

That's not to say these papers are insignificant—not in the least! In fact, I consider them to be the most important documents of all, since they include a much longer tale that took several years, or perhaps decades, for Kirschenbaum to pen—a tale, not merely of importance to understanding the ancient peoples of the Americas, but one which, if ever published, will serve to entirely overthrow the current views held by mainstream scientists of the history of the world. This longer tale, more importantly, strongly hints at why the bones of Kirschenbaum were never found—*nor likely to be found*, even if the Havasupai open their lands to further digs—though I resist the temptation to speak further on this matter until I have followed up on several clues left behind in the writings of Kirschenbaum.

Conclusion

Kirschenbaum, no doubt, intended his life to be shared with the world. In the journal entries you are about to read, note how frequently he addresses "children" and, occasionally, a child named "Avalon." Who Avalon and these other children were remains a mystery, but from the context, it seems likely they were residents of the mining camps. One may imagine the Miner 49er seated upon his trusty bucket beside a campfire, journal in hand, enthralling a group of children by reading aloud his adventures.

Without further ado on the origin and rediscovery of the journal of Cody Kirschenbaum, let us dive headlong into the pages of this man's remarkable life history. I present to you the raw, unvarnished writings in all their glory and occasional disarray, just as I found them. I took small liberties in providing titles to the journal entries, for the sake of indexing and referencing in archaeological publications, but I think you will find they do not detract from the message of the Good Miner; on the contrary, they frame the message.

I suspect that as I have been stirred to action in my own life by meditating upon these journal entries, you too will be challenged to hold up Kirschenbaum's life as a mirror to your own and, in comparison of your adventures, find deeper meaning in the past, greater hope in the future, and an unslakable thirst for the unknown, however far along that murky path his wisdom carries you.

Jack Dublin
Fall of 2017

1 MERQUEEN OF THE MISSISSIPPI (1851)

"So it was, as he stoked his campfire one evening, cooking up a right thick catfish he hooked that afternoon, he saw a sight appear on that black ribbon of the Mississippi that seemed almost magical—yea, it nearly stopped his heart for joy!"

As I remarked in journal entries past, Jacob Waltz, Sr and I came to be friends in a sluicing camp, when he lent me his boots to wear after I lost mine in a thunderstorm. Jacob Waltz and I shared several points in common, not least of which was the size of our feet, but also that we were both widowers, which means our beloved brides had passed on, and we were both struggling to rear young ones on our own.

I spoke of his boy Bubby to you'ns before, but I never got around to introducing his other, younger son, Ebenezer, whom everyone called Benny for short.

Now, I don't think it's out of place for me to mention that Jacob Waltz's bride, Delilah, came from a family of considerable wealth, so that when she passed away during the birth of Ebenezer, why, a sizeable fortune was willed on to Jacob, the lion's share of which was to be held in trust for the boys. But young Benny, always itchin' to see and do some new thing, wasn't content to wile away his youth in mining camps. No! In fact, all he ever seemed to talk about was exploring life along the mighty Mississippi River.

So, at the ripe old age of ten, Benny Waltz petitioned his father for his inheritance. Now, Benny was what you'd call a precocious child, seeing as he was as savvy in the wilderness survival arts as any plainsman or fur trapper. To anyone who spent more than ten seconds picking the young boy's brain, why, he was keen to find him socially adjusted and wise beyond his years. As much as Jacob resisted the idea of relinquishing the trust, he soon gave in, reasoning that Benny was less likely to find trouble when running free than when pinned down.

With his fortune tucked safely in his sock, Benny set off one spring morning to experience the life he yearned for on the Mississippi. Following trade routes back east, hitching rides on stagecoaches and cattle drives, he emerged from the dusty forsaken Southwest desert to find himself in the sweltering heart of Cajun country. Woo hoo—I do mean New Orleans!

Benny watched after each penny of his inheritance like a hawk watches after her young, buying only the essentials for an itinerant lifestyle—that is to say, the kind of life where he set down no roots, drifting hither and thither as his fancy carried him. He purchased such things as fishing line and hooks; a Sunday-best suit for attending church services and other social festivities; and a large tarpaulin to keep him dry from the frequent rains and morning dew. He purchased a sturdy roll of twine and a bucket of pitch, too, and with driftwood he foraged along the banks of the Mississippi, why, he did build himself a river-worthy raft.

He spent his days reclined on the raft—a little fishing, a little napping—and when he wasn't engaged in those leisurely activities, why, he'd tie the raft to the nearest tree and explore the wilderness. He'd hunt squirrels and rabbits out there with a slingshot, becoming quite the dead-eye—yea, perfecting an aim that would make even King David a tad envious.

In the evenings, he'd pitch tent in the wilderness, build a campfire, play songs on a harmonica and gaze into the great expanse of stars scattered 'cross the heavens above. Those were bar none the best days of his young life! 'Twould've remained that way, too, were it not for the fact that a restless boy like Benny couldn't stay put in one place for long—no! As I pointed out before, he was always looking on to the next thing, never content with the good life he had. So it was, as he stoked his campfire one evening, cooking up a right thick catfish he hooked that afternoon, he saw a sight appear on that black ribbon of the Mississippi that seemed almost magical— yea, it nearly stopped his heart for joy!

For in those days, large riverboats known as sternwheelers stroked their way up and down the Mississippi, with strains of trumpets, trombones and saxhorns billowing off their swag-splayed balconies, the decks lit bright as the Fourth of July. Onboard, gentlemen in tailcoats twirled beautiful young ladies arrayed in hoop-gowns—the kind of dresses that fanned out around the hips and puffed up like thunderclouds the faster the couples danced. 'Twas a carnival drifting by Benny's camp each evening, and it wasn't long before he got an itch to be a part of that twilight parade.

Now these sternwheelers carried folks along the river for entertainment purposes. And the type of entertainment of which I speak was gambling—poker tournaments, casting of dice and spinning the roulette wheel—all games of chance where the lucky winners stood to make a neat little fortune over the course of an evening; the losers, on the other hand, outnumbered the winners a thousand-to-one, and oft times lost the shirts off their backs—yea, the very last balls of lint out of their belly buttons! Now, don't you go laughing at that, thinking there ain't no value in belly button lint. Why, I saved up mine over the years and from it I knit together the shirt I'm wearing today. Indeed, 'tis the best shirt I ever owned.

But I'm getting ahead of myself telling you this story of Benny Waltz's adventures on the Mississippi. To be plain, this type of entertainment wasn't meant for children. So, Benny found himself in a bit of a pickle. How in tarnation was he supposed to gain entry onto the sternwheeler to participate in the nightly celebrations?

As Benny ruminated on these things, he sat down on a log and opened a can of sardines that he'd purchased at the general store—one of the few luxuries he afforded himself. Much to his surprise, as soon as he peeled back the lid of the can, why, he heard a gasp escape from inside—a gasp like one hears when a person comes up from being under water too long. It was *that* kind of gasp.

Turning the can toward the campfire, Benny peered inside, stirring his finger among the fish to pinpoint the source of the peculiar noise. No sooner had he done so than he saw something squirming inside, and out from the fish arose a sight that was quite hard for him to fathom—yea, for there among the sardines, slathered in mustard sauce, was a mermaid about the size of his thumb. And she was quite alive, no less.

She said, "Oh, thank you, thank you, thank you, Master for delivering me from this dreadful can. 'Twas nearly my tomb!"

"You're quite welcome. But dare I say, I can hardly believe my eyes. Are you a mermaid?"

"I am that type of creature that men would call a mermaid, but I am altogether much more than that." The little mermaid leaped from the can into the Mississippi River, where she rinsed the mustard sauce from her body. Then, she flipped out of the water and back into the can where she plucked a bone from a sardine to comb her catfish-black hair. The tresses shimmered like crude oil in the campfire light.

"How do you mean that you are much more than that—that is, a mermaid?"

"Why, I'm not just any mermaid, but I so happen to be the queen of the mermaids. My name is Delilah—Merqueen of the Mississippi."

"Your name is Delilah? That's my mammy's name! Well, 'twas before she died, anyhow."

"It's a beautiful name, if I do say so myself. But pray tell, what is my Master's name?"

"I reckon I don't know who your Master is, nor his name. As for me, my name is Benny."

"Pshaw—you have captured me! Therefore, you've become my Master until the day I grant you the third of three wishes, to which you are entitled."

"You grant wishes? I dare say you are pulling my leg, Delilah!"

"'Tis a fact. You may ask for anything, and I am bound by the code of the mermaids to convey it into your hands."

Benny thought about this for a moment. He had a good raft, he had the freedom to come and go this way and that as he pleased, and he even had his youth. Then it struck him. "I wish to be a part of the festivities on the sternwheeler, but I am only a boy. It is well known that young boys are not allowed onto the sternwheelers. And yet, that is my wish."

"As you wish, it will be so." Delilah curtsied to him. "But first, we must disguise you as a man."

The Merqueen leaped down from the sardine can into the darkness, rustling through Benny's belongings, making quite a ruckus for a creature so small. When she reemerged into the light, she sprang onto Benny's shoulder with a small bundling of grass blades, dipped in the pitch he used to waterproof his raft. She dabbed this on Benny's upper lip and chin, then pressed clumps of squirrel fur onto the pitch. She held up the shiny side of the sardine can lid for him as a mirror.

"Have a look, Master."

Benny gazed at his reflection on the lid and marveled at what he saw: a man round about the age of fifty years old! His heart skipped several beats, for he felt real hope of gaining entry onto the sternwheeler. Wasting not a moment, he changed out of his day-to-day clothes and into his Sunday-best suit, knowing the mustache and beard that Delilah fashioned for him was only part of the disguise. Once he was dressed, he placed Delilah in his pocket, untied the raft and paddled downstream for the sternwheeler dock.

No sooner had they reached the dock than Benny swaggered forward to pay the admission fee (it was a sizeable fee, to be sure, but Benny had brought his inheritance along, stuffed in his sock), but the closer he got to the boat, the colder his feet got for the ride. He stepped out of line and into the shadows, pulling Delilah the Merqueen from his pocket.

"I have another wish."

"As you wish, my Master."

"I wish that the people on this boat will like me. You know, treat me as someone special, like I'm someone important."

"As you wish, my Master."

And with that, Benny found his pluck, venturing forward to pay the admission fee, his disguise not raising the first question from the gatekeepers. In what seemed like a whirlwind of a moment, Benny was safely aboard the ship as the departure horn sounded, and the great churning of water from the sternwheel washed over the night. He had succeeded!

He pulled Delilah from his pocket, beaming at her. "We made it, Delilah! We made it! All thanks to you!"

"Not thanks to me," she corrected. "'Twas your rightful wish."

But no matter to Benny. He had come for adventure and adventure was brewing all about him. Elegant people passed by him, nodding and smiling. The expressions on their faces bespoke respect for him—indeed, pleasure to have glimpsed his appearance on the balcony of the ship! His heart swelled with pride, feeling he belonged on the ship, on that night, in that moment.

Benny pressed his way into the ballroom of the sternwheeler, tipping his hat to the piano player, swaggering past dancing, swirling couples and waiters carrying silver platters of hors d'oeuvres, slipping deeper into the heart of the vessel until at last he reached the gaming rooms. Now, listen up, children—Benny said, in my own presence, 'twas the greatest concentration of excitement he ever expected to behold this side of Paradise! He was drawn to the gaming table where dice were thrown for bets—that is, money was placed down on the table in wager that these or those numbers came up on the throws. Benny figured that was easy, seeing that he and his brother Bubby used to play dice in the mining camps.

He watched the games for a few moments before pulling Delilah from his pocket. "Listen," he told her. "Can I really wish for anything and you will grant it?"

"By the code of the mermaids, 'tis as you say."

"In that case, 'tis my final wish that I win $100,000 playing the dice table tonight. Can I really wish for that?"

Delilah made a little jump from his hand to his shoulder and whispered in his ear, "Of course, my former Master. With your third wish, I now bid you farewell."

And so it was that Delilah, Merqueen of the Mississippi, leaped from Benny's shoulder, flopped along the deck until she reached the railing, then disappeared over the edge into the night. Benny heard a little splash as she went down. Then, turning his attention to the dice table, he removed the inheritance from his sock and placed his wager on the line.

Now, I told you children that Benny's departed mother, Delilah, who so happened to share the same name as the Merqueen of the Mississippi, had left him a sizeable fortune in trust. But his inheritance was far less than $100,000, for that, dear children, is a sizeable amount of money indeed! Even so, he gambled his entire inheritance on a roll of the dice and a wish.

And do any of you children out there know what happened when Benny rolled the dice? Well, I imagine there are a couple of guesses out there as to what happened, but seeing as I'm not good at keeping secrets, why, I'll just tell you what happened. Benny won! Yes, indeed, he doubled his inheritance on a roll of the dice!

And the patrons on the ship that night treated Benny as someone special, as someone important, as he bought drinks for all those people in the room—to spread the wealth around, as it were. The patrons beloved Benny, indeed! So, he took what winnings remained after buying all those drinks and placed it back on the line.

And he rolled the dice.

And again, he won!

So, Benny, in the span of two rolls of the dice, had first doubled, and then quadrupled his winnings! Which is to say, he now had four times the inheritance with which he first stepped on board the sternwheeler. Why, it was just like the good times back in the mining camp, thought Benny, when he rolled the dice against Bubby for pickled herrings.

And at this point, doing some rapid mathematical calculations in his head, he realized he had won over $100,000! Enough money to set up him and his kinfolk for life—yea, for generations! But then, Benny thought, imagine what good double that amount could do? I think you all know the answer, don't you? Well, yes, that's right—it could do twice as much good!

With that thought fixed in his head, Benny placed his quadrupled inheritance on the line and rolled the dice. And do any of you children out there care to place a wager on what happened next?

Well, I don't want to take your money, and as I said before, I'm not so good at keeping secrets, so I'll just tell you. He lost it all! Yes, you heard right—young Benny, hero of the sternwheeler, friend of the patrons at the dice table, lost every penny he had on a single roll of the dice.

As the dealer pulled Benny's money off the table, a noticeable change came over the patrons. Their eyes turned away from Benny and the pats on his shoulders they gave freely only moments before did not return. 'Twere as if he wasn't even in the room! Well, 'twasn't entirely like that, seeing that security for the sternwheeler burst onto the deck at that moment, apprehending young Benny on charges of being a boy disguised as a man.

They shuttled him off to a dinghy, lowered him in the water and rowed ashore, where they left him on the banks to find his way back to wherever he had a mind to go.

Benny was crushed. How could he have been so careless with the inheritance left to him by his beloved mammy? As he sat on a log thinking about these things, behold, he heard a splashing in the river. In the moonlight, he saw Delilah, Merqueen of the Mississippi, climb onto a rock and toss back her inky locks of hair.

Benny glared. "You cheated me out of my wishes. You took me for everything I had."

"Did I?"

"You said you'd gain me entry to the sternwheeler but look at me now—tossed off the ship like a common stowaway!"

"But I did gain you entry."

"Well, what about my second wish, when I asked that all the people on the boat would like me, and treat me as someone special, as someone important. Where are they now?"

"And so they did treat you special, while you were winning and buying them things."

"But what about my third wish? I wished to win $100,000, but now I have nothing! How did you not cheat me out of that?"

"And so you did win $100,000, before you bet it all away." The Merqueen shook her head. "Such is life."

Benny knew Delilah was right. "But what am I to do now? Where am I to go?"

"Go home to your Pa. The face of a son always blesses a father, even one so wasteful with the inheritance entrusted to him."

With those words, Delilah—Merqueen of the Mississippi—slipped into the water and swam into the moonlit night, never to be seen by Ebenezer Waltz again.

Benny heeded her final advice, making his way out of the sweltering Cajun country, back into the dusty forsaken Southwest desert. It was a bright, clear morning when Benny stood in sight of the mining camp where his father and brother still lived. Much to his astonishment, he spotted his father in the distance, waving his hat high above his head. Then, his Pa was a running, running faster than he had ever run in his entire life to greet his son who was lost, but now was found.

When his Pa reached him, he wrapped him up in his arms, kissed him on the head and cried a good number of tears (the good kind of tears) for his son who had returned to him. Jacob Waltz, Sr, overjoyed by the return of Benny, called out all the prospectors and miners, all the foremen in the camp and all their families, to a celebration for the return of Benny. Why, he even bought up all the pickled herring in the camp for the celebration to follow.

But for all the joy in the camp that day, there was one resident who was not overjoyed—nay, Jacob Waltz, Jr, known to the world as Bubby, was about as sour and down in the dumps as one you ever saw. He sulked all day and into the evening shadows, refusing to celebrate, bitter that his Pa threw a great party for his brother who had wasted away his inheritance on a roll of the dice.

Old Jacob Waltz sought out Bubby and confronted him about his attitude. "Why are you not celebrating the return of your brother, who was lost but now is found?"

"Why should I? He doesn't deserve a party thrown in his name, with pickled herring as far as the eye can see—he squandered away his inheritance. As for me, I slave away like a dog in this camp with rags for clothes and blisters for wages, and not once have you thrown me a party."

"But Bubby, I always had you by my side, knowing you was safe. Your brother seemed lost and gone forever, only to return safely to my arms. You don't understand now, but one day you'll have your own children, and perhaps the distinction will be crystal clear to you then."

And with those words, Bubby's heart began to soften—yea, soften it did until he swallowed his pride and sought out his brother, falling into his arms and telling him how grateful he was to see him alive! Not to get too sappy on you, children, but those brothers did shed a few tears that evening, realizing how much they loved one another.

As they made amends, the tears gave way to smiles, the smiles gave way to laughter, and eventually Bubby said to his brother, "Hey, Benny. How about tossing me one of those pickled herrings?"

Benny, happy to do so, removed the lid from the herring box. But he found no pickled herrings, nor mermaids waiting to grant wishes. Instead, he found an empty box, not so much as a dollop of mustard sauce to be had. With a touch of sadness in his voice, he said, "Such is life."

Such is life indeed, children. For getting down to brass tacks, the moral of this story, the very crux of it, is that when we don't forgive others, we miss out on the good life. Or, as we like to say in the mining camp, *"Cut loose the saddlebags you've loaded up with sin, that you may pass out of the desert, through the narrow gate, and into the oasis of God."*

2 COYOTE IN THE MAIZE (1852)

"Rameses would scale the highest peak of the mountains on the darkest night of the month— when the moon slept, as legend had it—and snatch stars from the heavens, disfiguring the constellations thereof. The Indians said that what men often called shooting stars were nothing less than that crafty coyote thieving yet again."

After the drought of 1851, in which locusts descended on our camp and ate what meager crops we had eked out of the earth, a harsh winter followed that took many a lives in the sluicing camp. Yea, those of us who survived did so eating snowflakes for breakfast, icicles for lunch, and if we were lucky enough to net 'em out of the river, why, we'd enjoy frazil soup for dinner. Now do any of you children know what frazil are? Well, let me tell you—frazil are the chunks of ice formed in river rapids.

So, as you can readily deduce, all was not well for this 49er and his darling daughter Clementine. No! We were emaciated, downtrodden by the elements, and suffering from a touch of scurvy, to boot! As such, we packed up at the first thaw and made our way down from the mountains, into the Great Valley of California where crops where bountiful and rumor had it, gold was still being snatched out of the ground hand over fist!

We settled down a little to the northeast of Sacramento, in a mining camp named Hangtown. The town was so named for three common criminals hanged from the gallows in the early days of the camp. To be sure, it doesn't sound like any place you'd want to rear up a child, but the name was more about scaring away criminals than it was about the way things were. For you see, the reality was there hadn't been any hangings there since those three criminals, and the local church was working hard to change the name of the town to something that did not bespeak of death and lawlessness.

We enjoyed a comfortable existence in Hangtown that spring and summer. Plenty of work was to be had in the mines, and a prospector could still take his rocker—which is a box for separating gold from gravel—down to the river and make a little something extra in his spare time. As far as rearing Clementine went, why, she shared the company of a dozen children there in the camp which was uncommon during our travels—and furthermore, it meant that a schoolhouse was built in which to provide a goodly education for the young'uns.

Now, before I continue with the history of what happened in the camp that autumn, it is necessary to recount what was happening to the north of Hangtown, in Indian country, that same season. For you see, dear children, the Indians who lived up north at the base of the mountains had done so peacefully since the end of the ice age. But following the same harsh winter that drove me and Clementine to Hangtown, a trickster descended from the mountains who did upend the placid lives of the Indians—yea, I do mean one of the most cunning creatures who ever lived—a coyote by the name of Rameses.

For you see, Rameses would chase and nip at children while they played, warn deer to run when Indian hunting parties set out, and even tear the grass-woven walls off homes in the middle of the night, so that a cold breeze blew therein, causing the Indians to shiver, setting their teeth a chattering so loud that no one could sleep for the noise. And he would plunder any food they left out, too, such as acorn bread, smoked salmon and his favorite delicacy, salted rabbit.

Worst of all, Rameses would scale the highest peak of the mountains on the darkest night of the month—when the moon slept, as legend had it—and snatch stars from the heavens, disfiguring the constellations thereof. The Indians said that what men often called shooting stars were nothing less than that crafty coyote thieving yet again.

Now, you might ask yourselves, why on God's green earth and in His rivery blue heavens above would Rameses want to steal stars out of the sky? The answer to that, dear children, is that after he stole the stars, he hid the seeds of the stars, which are the rarest form of diamonds, known as

Galaxial diamonds, in caves all around the valley—yea, even beyond the valley—that he might return to them, time and again, to marvel after their beauty. You see, he wanted the beauty all to himself, not comprehending that the beauty of the stars was meant for the whole world.

The reckless ways of Rameses posed a major problem to the Indians, they said, because when he stole stars from constellations the world became imbalanced and destruction followed. Depending on which constellation he robbed, a different form of destruction ensued. For instance, when he stole a star from the constellation of the great Cohoes, the fishing season went poorly for the Indians. When he stole from the constellation of the great Water Bearer, drought and floods became common. Likewise, theft from the Hunter constellation ensured fewer deer and rabbits in the valley. In fact, many of the Indians swore that all ills in the natural world could be traced back to the perfidy of Rameses.

The distress in Indian country that spring of 1852 began as mild irritation but festered to gargantuan proportions as the coyote sowed his wild oats all about the valley. The Indians of the Great Valley, possessing the ingenious spirit they did, hatched a plan to thwart Rameses. To prevent the coyote from stealing any more of the stars, they expanded their fields of maize—that's what you children would call corn—all around the base of the mountain. The coyote, unable to see above the stalks to locate the mountain, became lost in the maize on the dark moonless nights when he hunted stars.

Rameses, in no way pleased by this reversal of fortune, entered the fields of maize during the day and bit down the stalks all the way to the base of the mountain, providing a clear path to the highest peak on those moonless nights.

As you can well imagine, the Indians found coexistence with Rameses to be an intolerable chore and thus they hatched another plan to rid him from the land once and for all. Their bravest warriors scoured the countryside for all the snakes they could find and released them into the fields of maize. The next time the coyote set paw into the maize to bite down the stalks, why, he was beset by a venomous brood of serpents that snapped at his heels, causing him to watch over his shoulder with every step. Unable to clear a path to the mountain, he became frustrated and vengeful.

Now, some of you children might be tempted to think that was the end of old Rameses—but you'd be wrong! For Rameses, being more cunning in the art of deception and destruction than the Indians were in stopping him, foiled their second plan in the cleverest of ways. You see, Rameses forged a pact with the crows, whereby he would lead them to the ripest ears of maize, if they agreed to tell him where the mice nested in the fields. Then, he forged another pact with the owls, that in exchange for revealing the location of the mice nests, they would guide Rameses with their screeches on those moonless nights to that highest of peaks, known as Golden Mountain. And that's exactly how Rameses continued to steal stars, wiping out entire constellations from the heavens in just a few short months.

To understand the devastation this caused the tribe, one must understand the purpose of constellations in the first place. You see, constellations were pictures by which the Indians told their children the history of the world, much the way we use books for the same end—so if the constellations lost their meaning, the Indians would forget their history. And as King Solomon once noted, what has been shall be again, and there is nothing new under the sun. But if you can't remember what happened in the past, then how can you prepare for the future?

As such, Rameses was causing far greater damage to the world than spoiling crops and thwarting hunts—yea, he was stealing the past! After one stole the past from the minds of the people, why, he was bound to insert an insidious lie in its place. Threatened with the loss of their history and the poisoning of their minds with lies, the tribal Elders raised the unthinkable specter of quitting the valley of their forefathers to seek out friendlier quarters in parts unknown.

I find it strange, dear children, how distress of this sort can muddle the minds of some, while emboldening the spirits of others. For you see, at the same time the tribal Elders were dead-set on relinquishing their birthrights on account of that menacing scoundrel of a canine Rameses, one boy among the tribe, not quite twelve years old, rose up to challenge the decision of the Elders. To see this boy, some might believe him to be the least among the Indians for his short stature and arms and legs so devoid of muscle, that they resembled spindles on a weaver's loom more than the limbs of a human being. As if those weren't two strikes against him in this tribe of proud warriors, why, he only had a single eye, an injury suffered at the beak of a falcon that swooped down upon him as he played in an open field as a toddler. Some of the older boys and younger men, bereft of all sympathies befitting godly men, teased him with the name Falcon Eye.

Now, before you go feeling sorry for this light-in-the-pants, one-eyed boy, you best understand that he never—not one day in all his years—felt sorry for himself. Nay! 'Twere a fact before the Living God that Falcon Eye trained his one remaining eye to see twice as well as any other man's best eye. He was fond of using a slingshot during the hunt, too, and because of his excellent vision, he could spy out and strike down a rabbit from over a mile away. Indeed, by such exploits, he came to redeem the name foisted upon him by men of mean character.

But for all the talents Falcon Eye possessed, he was still a young boy in the eyes of the Elders, meaning his opinion counted for next to nothing among them. So, when he stood up one evening amid the tribal council, urging man, woman and child to take the fight to Rameses, rather than turn tail and run, he was shouted down by the Elders and the warriors, causing his mother to break down in tears and cover her face for shame. Now, Falcon Eye had not meant to cause his mother pain, nor upset anyone, for that matter, but neither could he idle by as a knave coyote destroyed the peace and unity of his ancestral land.

Falcon Eye, ostracized by the community—which is to say, his friends and family wanted nothing to do with him—had no choice but to battle Rameses on his own. And so, he left the tribal council that night, wending his way through the valley until he reached the banks of a moonlit stream where he kneeled and cried out to Almighty God for strength in the coming war. When he arose from prayer, much to his surprise, he saw the shaman of his tribe—which is sort of like the Elder above all the other Elders—standing on the opposite bank of the stream. In his hand, he held a scroll which he extended to Falcon Eye.

"The prophecies of our ancestors foretold of this day," the shaman began, "when a trickster would steal so many stars from the heavens, that the constellations would be forgotten. But they also foretold of a boy who would recover the Galaxial diamonds, and set them back in their proper stations, that the world might flourish again. This scroll contains the ancient star maps, to aid you in your quest."

Falcon Eye, bewildered, accepted the scroll. "But what am I to do with this?"

"You will know when the time is right," the shaman said. "For now, choose five smooth stones from the stream and write the name of Rameses on each one. In your sling, they will express the power to bring the coyote down to earth."

Falcon Eye left the shaman on the bank of the stream and returned to the village where he bided his time. He studied the star maps and waited with his sling stones for the moon to sleep again. When that night finally came, he crouched at the edge of the maize field until Rameses arrived. Now, dear children, as I mentioned earlier, Falcon Eye had trained his one eye to see twice as sharp as any man's best eye, but what I didn't mention was that he also trained that eye to see in pitch blackness. So, even though Rameses, in times past, being soft upon his paws and guided by the screech of owls, eluded the serpents to reach the mountains beyond the maize, on this night the advantage belonged not to him.

Nay! As soon as Rameses entered the maize field, Falcon Eye began to sling stones his way. Rameses, mistaking the whizzing stones and rustling stalks for serpents, fell into a terrible state of confusion, whereby he also mistook his own tail for a snake, biting it clean off his behind! Now, to all who know the first thing about coyotes, they will tell you that his tail is his emblem of pride. And so, Rameses, thus humiliated, chose to flee Indian country lest he be teased for the remainder of his days.

The coyote's expulsion from Indian country, as Providence saw fit, brought him to the Hangtown mining camp in the autumn of 1852. Now, when Rameses first approached the camp toward sunset, why, who did he see walking along a path beside a stream with a basket in the crook of her arm, but my darling daughter, Clementine. Inside the basket, she carried sweet smelling biscuits, pickled herring, and a bottle of fresh goat's milk. The heavenly aroma stirred his belly and set it agrowl. This hunger crowded out all other thoughts until one remained: he must have that basket of goodies carried by the child. Lying down on the path, he waited for Clementine to approach. Then, taking in shallow breaths, he moaned as if felled by unimaginable pain.

Clementine gasped when she saw him on the path. But it was not a gasp of fright; rather, she took pity on him for his scrawny frame and missing tail. "You poor creature—what happened to your tail?"

Rameses blinked his eyes slowly several times before craning his neck toward Clementine. He said, "If I wasn't so parched from my travels and tribulations, I might tell you the whole sorry tale, no pun intended. But, as it stands, the mere thought of the ordeal is bringing on a case of the vapors.

"Please," he continued, "dip a cloth into the stream and ring some of the water into my mouth."

"'Twould be unchristianly of me to offer you only drops of water in your condition. You ought to drink from the source to your heart's content."

"Thank you, good child, but I am far too weak to walk to the stream." He altered his breath and moaned his discomfort. "'Twould take a far stronger drink than water to nourish me back to health. I fear I am ready to give up my breath to God who gave it."

And it was at that moment that Clementine, bless her heart, remembered about the bottle of milk in her basket. "Well, I do have this bottle of milk, but the thing is there is only one goat in this camp, so the milk is very expensive. Pop-pop panned a little extra gold out of the river this week and I wanted to surprise him with it. See, we ain't had milk since springtime."

"Sweet child, what is your name?"

"Clementine—or Clem, for short."

"And I am Rameses. Save the milk for you and your Pop-pop. 'Twould be unchristianly of me to take it."

And when she heard that, it took Clem no time at all to weigh the matter in her head. "No, I want you to have it, Rameses, for it would be unchristianly of me not to give the milk to you, a creature on death's door in need of nourishment."

Clementine held up Rameses' chin and poured a little milk into his mouth. She could see the brightness coming back into his eyes and it seemed his breathing did improve. Then, observing the dried blood on the stump of his tail, his mangy fur and scraped up paws, Clementine recalled her studies at the schoolhouse that day about caring for the least among us. "You really are quite a mess, aren't you? Let me clean and bind your wounds."

The coyote lifted his head slightly from the ground before dropping it into the dust.

Clementine made haste, tearing the pleated hem from her best school dress and binding the stump of his tail. Then, she fetched water from the stream and washed his ragged paws.

"You really shouldn't make such a fuss over me. Can't you see that I'm dying?"

"Dying? You mean like *dying* dying?"

"Yes, dying. Won't be long now—perhaps within the hour. 'Tis a certainty I have seen my last sunset." Then, turning his snout to the basket, Rameses sniffed the air, and sighed. "I smell pickled herring and sweet biscuits. Tell me if I am being impertinent, Clementine, but I fear I have only moments to live. To taste pickled herring and sweet biscuits a last time before I pass on to my reward would truly comfort my soul. It might even give me enough strength to tell you how I lost my tail."

"If it will comfort you in your last hour," Clementine said, brushing his mangy fur with her own hair brush, "far be it from me to withhold your dying wish."

And so, Clementine fed Rameses open-faced pickled herring biscuit sandwiches and poured milk into the corner of his mouth as he told her about his life in the valley, how he had lived there from the time he was a pup, until the Indians descended from the mountains and sowed weeds across the land, weeds that grew up so high as to blot out the mountain peak held sacred by all coyotes.

"What's worse, following the massacre at the Alamo, Davy Crockett fever swept the tribe. After decimating the racoon population, they hunted my kith and kin down for our tails—to make hats out of them!"

Clementine, being the sensitive soul she is, wept like an overflowing sluice. "How cruel—how infinitely and intolerably cruel! If you weren't dying, you could stay here, in Hangtown, without fear of being hunted down."

"Hangtown?" The concern rang sharp in his voice.

"Oh, it's just a silly name, to scare away the ruffians, the lawless and common thieves. The town council has not sentenced anyone to die in several years, for Hangtown is a rather peaceful, law-abiding mining camp these days. In fact, I travel this trail alone on my way to school and back, and I bring my ducks down to the water each morning. Had I felt in danger at any time, I would never be so bold."

"You have ducks?"

"Oh, yes. Seven of the most lovable creatures you ever laid eyes on, which produce enough eggs for Pop-pop and me. Would that I had more!"

"Oh, yes!" Rameses salivated. "Would you had more!"

The last of the color faded from the sky and the first stars peaked through the veil of dusk. Clementine finished brushing Rameses' fur, then turned to place the hair brush back into the basket. Lo-and-behold, the basket was empty!

"Oh, no! The food was meant for dinner this evening. Pop-pop will feel greatly abused when I return empty-handed. What am I to do?"

Before Rameses could answer, a lantern light appeared at the far end of the trail, and a faint voice called out for Clementine, echoing throughout the valley.

"It's Pop-pop!"

The coyote bolted upright, quite to Clementine's surprise, for his sudden health and agility did not befit the enfeebled creature she encountered only an hour before. He scurried off the trail behind a bush.

"Rameses!" She stepped to the brush line, but seeing Rameses' eyes glinting through the sage, she retreated a step. "You played on my emotions—you said you were dying!"

"And so I was dying... dying to eat your basket of goodies. But please, don't despise me for yielding to my temptation. I will repay what I have eaten in gold, for I have traveled this valley far and wide, and I know where vast deposits are to be found. Meet me here, tomorrow morning, and I will deliver on my promise. Farewell, Clementine!" And with that, he slinked into the shadows, leaving Clem alone, hungry and ashamed.

Now, dear children, don't be surprised to learn that when I found Clementine on the trail by the river, her basket and her belly empty, she lied to my face about the entire incident. Yes, indeed! She said she lost the money along the trail and had been fruitlessly searching in the dark for the coins. For shame has caused many to stumble in this world, and Clementine was no different.

You see, in her heart she reasoned that if Rameses delivered on his promise, why, the incident could be swept under the rug with none the wiser. That said, she resolved to meet Rameses the next morning in the false hope that he would make good on his promise. Fact is, Rameses didn't know the first thing about deposits of gold any more than he knew how to find his way to a mountain from the middle of the maize. No! And the further fact is, I think Clementine knew he didn't know any of this, but she had a soft spot in her soul for those in need of the Gospel, and she aimed to live it out before his eyes, even if it meant, as it did that night, she went to bed hungry while his belly was full.

For Clem remembered the proverb of Solomon, which says, "If your enemy is hungry, give him food to eat. If he is thirsty, give him water to drink. For in so doing, you will heap burning coals upon his head, and the Lord will reward you." In the mind of my darling daughter, doing all those lowly things for Rameses was an act of love, that he might be convicted of his selfish ways and turn his heart to God. But she would soon come to understand that loving her enemy was downright difficult, for to heap those burning coals upon his head, she must first carry them in her own hands.

Clementine arose the next morning and led her seven ducks to the stream, as she always did, round about nine, before the school bell rang.

Rameses awaited her on the path, gripping a shiny nugget of gold in his paws. "Come and see—I have made good on my promise and more! I have found a deposit beyond the ridge, a little south of here."

Clementine marveled at the size of the nugget Rameses held in his paws. She followed him along the stream, down through a canyon which led beyond the ridge of which Rameses spoke. But when they reached the place that Rameses claimed was awash in gold, Clementine sighed for his error. She had been around mining camps long enough to know the shiny yellow flakes were not gold at all, but pyrite—what miners liked to call fool's gold.

"But is this not a nugget of gold?"

Clementine examined the nugget he held and could not deny it. "'Tis bona fide gold."

"Then I have simply misremembered where the deposit lies."

In the distance, Clementine heard the pealing of school bells, announcing the commencement of morning lessons. She bemoaned that she would be tardy to class, having yet to water the ducks and return them to their coup. Rameses, ever the gentleman, promised to finish the task on her behalf.

"And afterwards, I will return here, to locate the deposit from which I found this bona fide nugget of gold."

Reluctantly, Clementine agreed, fearing the rapping across the knuckles she would receive from the schoolmarm if she tarried.

After school, Clementine returned to the river where Rameses led the ducks. He was reclined against a log, looking sleepy, his belly very fat, cleaning his teeth with a duck quill. Clementine cried, "You promised to lead them to the river!"

"Yes, so I did—I thoroughly enjoy a drink of cold water after a warm breakfast," he said, patting his belly.

"But I loved them!"

"And I loved them too—so much so that I ate them, that they would be part of me forever!"

Clementine wept bitterly for her loss. "The eggs are our primary source of food—indeed, the seven eggs laid this morning are all we have left. When they are gone, what ghastly fate knocks at our door?"

Rameses, feeling some peculiar sensation in his innards, like the untrained strumming of a banjo ('twas remorse!) promised to repay in gold for the ducks he ate. "For I have traveled this valley far and wide, and I know where vast deposits of gold are to be found. You shall then afford seven times seventy ducklings if you please. Or even a goat!"

But the only gold deposits Rameses knew about resided in the possession of men. Thus, later that day, when Rameses was caught stealing gold from the camp grounds, a Hangtown posse marched him straightaway to the gallows. Urged onward by his captors to the platform, Rameses came to understand that truism penned by the distinguished man of letters, Samuel Johnson, when he wrote, "The gallows doth wonderfully concentrate the mind."

Yea, they do indeed!

Clementine was on her way to school at that moment and, as Providence saw fit, witnessed the commotion. She beheld Rameses on the platform, a noose of seven knots fastened 'round his neck, begging for leniency and life. And Clem, being the delicate soul she is, intervened. Some women from the local church came alongside, asking the authorities for what the town should be remembered? More hangings, or better angels?

The miners protested. "God may forgive his sins, but who will make good on the fortune he stole? His neck for our gold!"

Clementine shouted above the din, "I will make good!"

A hush fell over the crowd as Clementine approached the miner who had called for Rameses's neck, opening the basket in her arms. "Please, take these seven duck eggs. 'Tis all I have." The women of the church stepped forward, too, loosening the clasps of their purses to fatten the ransom, and soon a gentleman's hat was passed around the crowd for an offering.

The town council deliberated, and then agreed, with the assent of the robbed miners, that Rameses go free, on the condition that his banishment from Hangtown extend to the remainder of his days; should he return, every man, woman and child was granted license to shoot on sight.

It passed that after Clementine and the church ladies ransomed the coyote from the gallows, he returned to the Indians who had shunned him, begged their forgiveness, and vowed to live in harmony with them from that day forward. Indeed, old Rameses entered the fields to fetch their maize, a job which they despised after releasing the snakes therein; for you see, the snakes were no respecters of persons, snapping at coyotes and Indians alike. And yet, Rameses fetched maize with a joyful heart, knowing that his actions had become a blessing to the community, rather than a curse.

And even though he couldn't see the mountain peak from which he once leaped to steal stars from the heavens, from the edge of the cornfield where he laid down at night, he could see the homes of the Indians, and the way the mothers and fathers, freed from their toil in the fields of maize, now re-purposed that time to play with their children and tell stories and laugh, all the while experiencing the deep satisfaction of knowing one's burden has been lifted.

As for Rameses, he didn't feel he had taken on their burdens at all. Nay! He felt the joy that flows to all who seek to serve rather than to be served. And seeking to serve, he reconciled with Falcon Eye, too, so that in time, Rameses and the boy journeyed throughout the valley, gathering the Galaxial diamonds and carrying them back to Golden Mountain. From the peak, Falcon Eye consulted the ancient star maps, loaded each star seed into his sling and launched them to their proper stations in the heavens. And it followed, dear children, that the world began to flourish again.

So, getting down to brass tacks, the moral of this story, the very crux of it, is that you should do unto others as you want them to do unto you. Or, as a fellow once said in a mining camp up north, *"Don't seek your fortune only to get ahead. And don't puff up with pride when you grasp that nugget of gold—instead, be humble, and reap a greater reward."*

3 THE GREAT GREAT PLAINS FIRE OF 1824

"The hungry flames threatened to devour White Stockings and Cody's homesteads, sending all the folks into a tither, running this way and that, carrying on like they didn't have the sense God gave a rabbit."

Way back in the year 1824, before I met my lovely bride Millicent, who bore us our darling daughter Clementine, a raging fire swept across the plains, forcing the Indians and the white man—who in times past had been at war with one another—to band together to fight the conflagration that threatened their homesteads; yea, their very lives! And the bravest among these Indians was a boy who stood only so high, no older than six years old, who had been given the name White Stockings.

Now, you might not think that sounds like any Indian name you ever heard—and you'd be right! But 'twas the name given to him by his tribal elders for the pair of stockings he was fond of wearing, a pair of stockings handed down to him by his great, great grandpappy Squinting Eagle. Squinting Eagle, you see, came upon the stockings by way of a French fur trapper who passed that way back in the year 1702, long before the United States of America—the land in which we live—was even a country!

Let me tell you, Miss Avalon, these white stockings were the finest pair of socks you ever laid your dreamy little eyes upon. They were long enough for a man to pull up to just under his knees, with fancy balls of yarn stitched into the hem, round about here, that rollicked like fairies when you walked in them.

The French fur trapper loved those white stockings nearly to the point of death, seeing as they were a gift from his mammy, who knitted them for young Frenchie just before he set sail for the New World in search of his fortune. All of which is to say, only the direst of circumstances could cause him to part ways with that most treasured gift. But Frenchie found himself in a quite a pickle that harsh winter of 1702, out on the desolate plains, and seeing that he had no food, but the Indians did, why, he arranged an exchange of a three-month supply of salted venison, which is deer meat, and a grab-bag of dried vegetables for his beloved, exquisite, *sui generis* stockings. So, while Frenchie ruefully parted ways with the stockings, the exchange of food saved him from certain death; thus, the socks had served their great purpose in his life. He comforted himself and his cold, naked shins with the knowledge that those white wool stockings, knit together by his mammy in the homeland, had gone out with blessings of life to another person on this great big rock we call the world, counted number three from the Sun.

Squinting Eagle, on the other hand, was a man who knew a thing of great value when he saw it, and those stockings were about the most valuable earthly possession he had ever laid his greedy hands upon. He was more than happy to help young Frenchie out of a jam by taking possession of the socks, but it wasn't charity that stirred his heart to make an exchange with the fur trapper—no! He had an ulterior motive, which is to say he was doing it for a different, secret reason. You see, Squinting Eagle imagined those were no ordinary socks—with the dangling balls of yarn stitched into them, dancing like fairies in the moonlight just before the harvest—but quite possibly they were magical socks, capable of making the wearer thereof fleet-footed, long of life and wealthy beyond all his wildest imaginations!

Which brings us back to White Stockings, who inherited those precious socks from his great, great grandpappy. In the springtime before the great fire, White Stockings befriended a boy of his same age, a settler by the name of Cody Kirschenbaum, whose family had emigrated from the Germanic lands several years earlier. The friendship caused no small disagreement between the clans of those two boys. You see, while the settlers and the Indians by that time had more or less learned to live in peace side by side, there persisted a certain amount of distrust between the peoples, so that any direct interaction across the family lines was anathema—which means, Miss Avalon, that the friendship between the boys was hated, detested, loathed and despised by the families.

While the families discouraged the friendship between the boys, why, they could hardly forbid such a thing, seeing that both boys spent a good deal of time swimming, fishing and fetching drinking water from the same river that separated their homesteads. And as you might have already guessed, seeing that they lived just next door to each other, they soon set out exploring the surrounding lands together, fashioning fishing hooks and lures from wire and bird feathers, constructing slingshots from cattle bones and catguts, and even making kites from deer skin leather. Those were bar none the best days of their young lives!

It wouldn't always be like that, though, as you soon shall hear.

You see, that summer was terribly dry, so dry, in fact, that the water level dropped in the stream, falling lower and lower, like a draining bathtub, until White Stockings and Cody could no longer swim there. In fact, when they dipped their pails in the stream to fetch water each morning, they often came up with more mud than water. It was under these desiccated conditions, in the month of September, that a dry thunderstorm arose—that is to say, there were plenty of dark, fat cumulonimbus clouds in the sky, but it was so dry that the rain that fell out of those clouds evaporated before it ever hit the ground. Oh, if only it had reached the ground— everything might have turned out differently. But as it was, only lightning reached the ground, sparking a fierce and terrible blaze that young children remembered the rest of their lives and when they grew old, they told the history of it to their children, grandchildren and great grandchildren—just like I'm telling you here today!

Flames chewed up acre upon acre of grassland, racing along the plains, driven by a strong western wind that accompanied the thunderstorm. Smoke filled the air so thick that it darkened the noonday sun and you had to wear a wet handkerchief across your nose and mouth just to breathe. Fire filled the horizon from east to west and north to south, so that no matter which direction you set your squinting, burning eyes, it looked like you were in the midst of a great bowl of fire. Nightmare of nightmares, there was nowhere to run.

The hungry flames threatened to devour White Stockings and Cody's homesteads, sending all the folks into a tither, running this way and that, carrying on like they didn't have the sense God gave a rabbit. So, White Stockings' father and Cody's father both ran faster than they had ever run in their entire lives along the banks of the stream to the western border of their homesteads, trying to gauge how long they had before the conflagration overtook them.

To understand what happened next, it's helpful to describe the layout of the homesteads belonging to the two families. White Stockings land and Cody's land lay on opposite sides of the river from each other, as you know, but what you don't know is that toward that western boundary, the river angled to the north, meaning the path of the fire would intersect White Stockings homestead before it ever reached Cody's homestead.

So, White Stockings' father looked across the river to Cody's father and said, "Neighbor, help me cut back the grass, douse the soil with whatever water we have and shepherd my livestock downwind."

But Cody's father said, "I cannot, lest while I help you cut back the grass, douse the soil and shepherd your livestock downwind, the wind should change direction and carry the flames onto my homestead, destroying all that I have. I must make the preparations you name for my own family. You, sir, prepare your own kinfolk."

"There isn't time for us to prepare alone. Besides, as soon as you finish helping me defend my homestead, me and my kinfolk will help to defend your homestead."

"When have you ever helped me? No, I fear you are trying to trick me, and that after I help defend your homestead, you will abandon me and my kinfolk to the flames of perdition. Therefore, I will not help you."

White Stockings' father resented the accusations made against him. He pointed a calloused, trembling finger at his neighbor. "Look, man, should I return evil for good? Everything is lost for me without your help, and all is lost for you without my help, so we must help each other. Besides, the fire is bound to consume my homestead before yours, so if I perish in this blaze, so shall you!"

And back and forth the two men bickered like this for a quarter hour, each refusing to budge, each convinced in his own eyes that he was right. It was sin, plain and simple—the deceitful sin of pride—that the two men could not compromise at that crucial moment. But the fire would not wait for the men to settle their disagreement and, indeed, it drew dangerously close while they chose to argue rather than compromise, so much so that at last the two men dropped to their knees, crying out to Almighty God for His blessing of deliverance.

Now, White Stockings and Cody had run up the banks of the river to witness the petty argument between their fathers, and they had had just about enough of it. They could smell the very hairs on their heads smoldering and knew something had to be done that very minute and not one second later. It was then that Cody recalled, earlier in the summer, that he and White Stockings had ventured to the east, about a half-day walk, following the river to discover its source. While they didn't uncover that mystery, they did come upon quite a sight, a sight that might well explain—at least in part—why the river ran so dry into September. You see, off there to the east, a very eager beaver had chewed down some trees and built himself a dam in that stream, so that on the one side of his dam water trickled to Cody and White Stocking's homesteads, but on the other side it swelled into a deep, refreshing pool the beaver frolicked in to his heart's content.

Cody called out to White Stockings. "We must get to the beaver dam and tear it to pieces! Perhaps the resultant surge of water will quench this infernal blaze and save us all!"

White Stockings knew Cody was right, but the beaver dam was a half-day walk away. How could they get there fast enough to execute the plan and save their homesteads? It was at that moment that White Stockings remembered how his great, great grandpappy, Squinting Eagle had once said the stockings that White Stockings wore were capable of making a man fleet-footed. But even if the legend was true, White Stockings could not tear the dam to pieces by himself. He would need Cody's strength, working in concert with his own, to succeed. So, White Stockings peeled off one of his stockings—the great inheritance received from his forefathers—and tossed it across the river to Cody. "Put on the white stocking," he shouted. "It will make you fleet-footed—fleet-footed enough to reach the dam in time to carry out your plan."

Cody slipped his toes into the soft and welcoming sheath of the ancient sock, and he felt a tingle run up his leg. It was the tingle of power—almost like an electric current—

encouraging Cody's feet to run. Knowing time was not on their side, the boys set off on a dead sprint for the beaver dam. It seemed they ran faster than the wind itself, and if it be believed, why, they swore their feet never touched the ground, almost as if they flew the entire way. They wasted not an instant at the dam, rending those great logs into splinters, unleashing a mighty torrent of water on the plains not seen since the Great Flood of old—nay, not even until this day. And the waters performed the task the boys released them to do, dousing all the flames and saving the homesteads.

White Stockings and Cody raced back along the river the way they had come—floating on air, it seemed—until they reached their families, falling into the arms of their mothers and brothers and sisters. They were lifted on the shoulders of their relatives, heralded as heroes, and the two clans vowed to help each other from that day forward until the very last star fell from the sky.

The stockings—knit together in a bygone age by a loving mother for her son—once again delivered blessings of life. As for Squinting Eagle's assessment of the magical properties of the socks... did they make the wearers thereof fleet-footed? Indeed, fast enough to reach a far off, pesky beaver dam in the nick of time. Did they make the wearers thereof long of life? Well, what life is longer than the life that lives to see another day! And did they deliver wealth beyond one's wildest imaginations? Oh, dear child, what greater wealth is there than neighbors dwelling together in harmony!

But for every happy ending, there is a sad ending, too. For you see, Miss Avalon, White Stockings and Cody's fathers did not survive the conflagration that swept the plains in September of 1824. Those two bickering fools allowed pride to cloud their judgment, and it cost them dearly—yea, their very lives!

So, getting down to brass tacks, the moral of this story, the very crux of it, is we must *"encourage each other every chance we get, lest our hearts become hardened by the deceitfulness of sin."* And that bit of wisdom, as you may know, and I'm certain you do since you're sharp as a bullwhip, comes straight from the Good Book itself, Hebrews 3:13 to be precise.

4 THE LOST CONTINENT OF
HORATIO SWANFIRE (1831)

"*Captain Humdinger climbed onto the prow, with a steely gaze set upon the sea ahead, and ordered his crew to open the third sail. As the sail caught wind, lurching the ship forward, he bellowed into the burst of seafoam, 'Give me treasure or give me death!'*"

For the better part of my life, dear children, my *raison d'être*—which is the fancy French way of saying the very reason that I existed—was to strike my fortune anyway I knew how, be it sailing the high seas in hurricanes, repelling down volcanoes that were fixing to blow their tops or mining the depths of the earth during a dynamite explosion.

Twasn't until I reached the grandfatherly state in which you see me today that I had reason to reflect on the fact that for all that searching for fortune I'd done, I had nothing tangible—nothing I could hold in my hands—to show for it. Why, the only thing I salvaged through the years were the memories I'd jotted down of the dumb and dangerous things I'd done in search of those riches. And so, it seems good to me to share another tale with you today from my journal; a tale about the lost continent of Horatio Swanfire.

Back in the year 1831, round about the time I finished the eighth grade—which in those days was all the schooling a boy could hope to get if he was growing up on a farm, like I was—I set out for the Yucatan Peninsula in Mexico searching for a little bit of gold, and a bigger bit of adventure.

And so it was that I found my way to the ancient Mayan city of Chichen-Itza, where, if the rumors were to be believed, I could find work as a day laborer excavating that architectural wonder known as the Kukulkan pyramid.

Well, the rumors in this case bore much fruit, as a team of archeologists from one of those highfalutin Ivy League universities in the Northeast, led by a hard-driving, treasure-seeking professor by the name of Jasper Gypsum, hired me on as a shovel-and-pick boy—which is to say, I was fixing to earn me some blisters and sunburns under the fierce Mexican sun!

Now, if all I found were blisters and sunburns, this wouldn't be much of a story, now would it? No! It would be one of the sorriest stories you ever did hear. But I'm here to tell you we found much more than that. Yea, 'twas toward the end of an uneventful, backbreaking day—a little before sunset—that we uncovered a large slab of stone inscribed with strange markings of an unknown language.

In that moment when the alpenglow settles upon the earth—that is, when the last rays of sunlight peek around the corner of the globe and everything seems to turn to gold—we hitched a team of horses to that mighty slab and dragged it aside, and yea, we discovered a hidden chamber lay beneath it!

At the sight of this, why, Professor Gypsum ordered the lighting of torches and the lowering of a ladder into the chamber, eager to discover at once what riches lay below. We descended into the chamber not knowing if it was a vault full of riches or the tomb of an ancient king!

But here's where the story gets mighty interesting, children, so I want you to lean in close when I tell you this: lined up on the floor of that room were seven exquisitely painted jars—artwork to compare with the great Michelangelo of old! But if that don't pique your interest, then let me tell you what we found inside those jars was enough to cause Professor Gypsum's eyes, in the flickering torchlight, to blaze with unrestrained gold fever!

The Professor's jaw hung slack—way down to about here—as he removed from the jars scrolls with unbroken seals, scrolls unread since the time their words were set to papyrus with ink! Tentatively, he broke the first seal, revealing what even a farm boy with an eighth grade education could plainly see—'twas a treasure map!

But, to simply call it a treasure map would be a great disservice to this tale, for the detailed rendering of the Gulf of Mexico contained a vast, circular island in the midst thereof—with canals and cities and pyramids—that any present-day fisherman can tell you don't exist. More inscriptions of that unknown language tattooed the scroll, which the Professor believed told the history of how the island had vanished in the sea.

Now, I'm certain many of you children here today will draw the same conclusion that Professor Gypsum drew there in the torch-lit recesses of that chamber—yea, that the map held in his hands marked the way to the lost civilization of Atlantis!

The professor wasted no time in raising the jars and the scrolls from the chamber and shuttling them off to a safe location. Then, utilizing his university connections, and no small amount of gold and silver coins, he secured a meeting with an expert in ancient languages that very night.

The expert inspected the maps and determined the unknown language was an ancient variation of the Mayan language, and as such, he could decipher for us the contents of the scrolls. Here is what we learned:

In the days before Noah's flood, two great kingdoms ruled the world. The first kingdom, rooted on an island in the Gulf of Mexico, was named Atlantis, with its capital city Atlas. The second kingdom centered on a vanished land off the African coast, called Lemuria—named for the tiny, wild monkeys that scampered in the jungles thereof. Now these kingdoms rose to preeminence among the nations but found themselves vying for similar resources. Soon, they became mortal enemies, and war did follow.

Each kingdom had utterly abandoned their reliance on God Almighty and instead desired more and more for themselves—never satisfied—resorting, in the final days, to launching vast armadas of ships to pillage the lands of weaker peoples, to bring back whatever resources they could stuff in the hulls of their ships.

Now, the Lemurians were for the most part shepherds and farmers—dealing in wool, cedar and grains—and enjoyed wiling away the nights by dreaming up constellations from the stars in the sky and creating stories to explain those constellations. In contrast, the Atlanteans prided themselves as miners, chemists and scientists who wrestled with the unknown world to understand it, asking large questions about why the planets moved this way and that, and why it seemed the stars shifted in the heavens from season to season.

As soldiers, the Lemurians were fierce men of war who trained themselves by fighting the world around them. Yes, indeed—when I say they fought the world around them, I don't mean they fought their neighbors, I mean they would attack hillsides, throw themselves into blackberry bushes, or they would kick and punch mountains as hard as they could until it hurt too much to kick and punch anymore, and at that point they would bite the bark off trees, just to show the world it couldn't get the better of them.

The Atlanteans, on the other hand, thought the Lemurians were crazy, and they fashioned weapons of war from all the metal they mined. They were skilled swordsmen—as skilled, if not more, than the samurai; and they were scientists, too, with the greatest scientist among them serving as their supreme leader, who reigned from the city of Atlas. His name was Horatio Swanfire.

Now, besides being a leader, Horatio Swanfire was an inventor. As far as his inventions went—well, some were works of genius, such as the wheel; others were works of doubtful use, such as the rubber chicken; and some were just plain dangerous, as the scrolls were about to reveal.

The language expert interpreting the scrolls for Professor Gypsum told us of the final days of Atlantis. You see, children, it seems Horatio Swanfire suspected the Lemurians were planning an invasion to end all invasions, one that would culminate with the Lemurians ruling the planet both far and wide. It stands to reason that if you had enemies across the sea, you wouldn't want them being enemies in your own land, so you'd think up a strategy to keep them rapscallions at bay. And I'm here to tell you that old Swanfire devised a plan to attain that very goal!

You see, Horatio concocted a mixture of chemicals which, when exposed to a spark or open flame, exploded with the force of a volcano! Horatio's compound is the same compound we call gunpowder. but back then they called it Swanfire dust.

I mentioned before that the island of Atlantis was more or less a circle, bordered by walls a hundred feet thick and a hundred feet high, designed to keep the Lemurians outside. This is important because Horatio's plan, you see, was to pile up his gunpowder all over the capital city of Atlas, then balance a huge ball of gold on the city walls to create a weapon akin to a cannon. But when I say that ball of gold was huge, I do mean to say, children, it was quite nearly the size of the moon!

Horatio performed some advanced mathematical calculations and determined that with just the right amount of gunpowder packed into the city walls—in direct proportion to the mass of the gold ball balanced on the city walls—why, an explosion would generate sufficient force to launch that projectile into low earth orbit, carry it briefly around the planet, then fall at a terrific speed and dash Lemuria to smithereens. Horatio reckoned if his enemies saw the ball of gold in the sky, they wouldn't even think of escaping—no! They'd mistake it for the noonday sun and just go about their business as if a giant cannon ball weren't fixing to pulverize their land.

For all the brilliance of Mr. Swanfire, he failed to consider an important fact: if the plan executed to form, why, the Lemurians would look up and behold not one shimmering orb in the sky, but two, and his carefully crafted legerdemain—that is to say, his trickery—would be plainly exposed for all who had eyes to see and they'd flee!

But that proved not to be the fatal flaw in Swanfire's ill-conceived plan. No! 'Twas the fact that none of the Atlanteans followed after God, but only did what was right in their own eyes. As such, the businessman Horatio contracted to mix the gunpowder realized he could improve his profits if he trebled the amount of charcoal in Swanfire's compound.

While this increased the man's profits, it also weakened the explosiveness of the gunpowder—sort of like if you don't add enough chocolate to milk, you get weak-tasting chocolate milk!

Needless to say, children, the scheme of Horatio Swanfire did not go as planned. When the men of Atlas ignited the charcoal-heavy gunpowder, the golden cannon ball shot a mile high in the sky, but no further, then plummeted—in an unwavering straight line—with the same force it had risen.

All of this is to say, when you drop a metal ball the size of the moon onto a city from a mile high, why, tragic consequences do follow. And so it was with the firing of Horatio's cannon—yea, it did bring about the sinking of an entire continent and the destruction of a people who did not know how to be content with what they had.

When the language expert finished his translation, Professor Gypsum rallied our band of archeologists in search of a ship we might hire to find the lost continent of Horatio Swanfire. For you see, the Professor surmised that if a ball of gold the size of the moon sank an island in the Gulf, why, a good portion of that gold ought to be lying there on the seafloor, waiting for him to scoop it up!

In short order, we enlisted the aid of the captain of a three-masted ship, a man by the name of Harry Humdinger, who, we would learn, possessed an even greater zeal for the treasure hunt than did Professor Gypsum.

We set out onto the Gulf of Mexico at sunrise, a steady wind blowing us on two masts toward the north, a hunger for gold burning in our bellies! Yea, Captain Humdinger, while ignorant of the treasure maps and history of the people who lived there in antediluvian times—that is, the time before the flood—nonetheless, caught scent of the gold fever burning within us. He climbed onto the prow, with a steely gaze set upon the sea ahead, and ordered his crew to open the third sail. As the sail caught wind, lurching the ship forward, he bellowed into the burst of seafoam: "Give me treasure, or give me death!"

And so it was, our fateful journey was underway.

But children, the Gulf of Mexico is no insignificant body of water—nay! There be over 660 quadrillion gallons of water in that thar sea, so to say we had our work cut out for us is akin to saying you might experience some issues teaching a fish to ride a bicycle.

Well, we were a young crew, a foolish crew, caught up in the gold fever that Professor Jasper Gypsum and Captain Harry Humdinger stoked deep down in our innards, and we weren't about to let several hundred quadrillion gallons of water impede our quest for riches. No! We aimed to sail forth into the sea—smack dab to its center—then dive down and see what treasures awaited us.

Once we reached the center, Captain Humdinger dropped anchor, and we drew straws to determine which lucky fellow would make the maiden dive to the Atlantean ruins. Lo-and-behold, children, the lot fell to yours truly. So, I tied one end of a rope to the ship's mast and the other end to my favorite ankle—which be the right one—and placed my trusty bucket over my head.

Now, you might ask why I would place a bucket over my head, and the reason has a scientific explanation. So let me ask you, children: how many of you have ever placed a wad of cotton or some such thing into a cup, then turned that cup upside down and plunged it into a bucket of water? Well, what happens to the cotton?

That's right, the answer is nothing! It don't get any wetter than it was when you first stuffed it into the cup, and that's because the air pressure prevents any water from getting inside the cup. The bucket on the head trick, then, achieves the same result, and serves as a poor man's diving gear.

Now, don't go trying that at home, children— otherwise you're liable to get yourselves killed! Yes, indeed! We don't need no one drowning themselves trying to replicate some stupid thing I did when I was just a young boy lacking any common sense. Are we clear on that point?

Good, because it was a downright dumb idea from the beginning, and one that nearly got me killed! For you see, in order to submerge myself beneath the water with the bucket over my head, the crew convinced me I needed to tie a sandbag to my least favorite ankle to counteract the buoyancy of the bucket. That way, I could sink all the way down to the

Atlantean ruins and the fields of gold that most certainly lay in the deep.

There were two major problems with this plan: number one, when I sank down to the bottom of the sea, with this metal bucket over my head, why I couldn't see a blasted thing—no!—nothing but my feet directly under me; number two, and this was the real kicker, it didn't dawn on me 'til I was a hundred feet under the sea that in order to loosen the sandbag from my ankle, I'd have to let go of the bucket!

Well, this presented me with no small quandary, seeing that as soon as I released the bucket, it felt like the weight of the sea did smack me upside the head and I came close to losing the breath out of my lungs! Also, one of the well-meaning ship hands—well-schooled in the art of tying knots—had secured a knot on my ankle that just wouldn't come undone.

But still having some measure of wits about me, I thrust my hand in the sediment below, searching for something like a rock or seashell, reckoning I could use it to tear open the sandbag. And so it was, as I dug in the sediment, that I did find a seashell with which to cut open the bag. But more importantly, having cleared the sediment aside, I glimpsed the unmistakable shimmer of solid gold there on the ocean floor!

This got me cutting at the bag with all the alacrity I could muster, and as the sand spilled out of the bag I shot up to the surface of the Gulf like a cork out of a bottle! The crew fished me and my trusty bucket from the water, eager to hear what I'd found.

"Gold!" I shouted. "Miles of pure gold!"

Professor Gypsum, at last, came clean to Captain Humdinger about the maps and the history of the city of

Atlas. After a brief consultation, they concluded that what I'd seen down below represented either the entire ball of gold that Swanfire blasted into the sky, or a large portion thereof. Either way, the only way we could carry any of it back was to blast it into smaller pieces.

And so it was, with bucket on my head, sandbag on my ankle, seashell in my teeth and waterproof dynamite in my hand, that I jumped back into the waters to lay the charge to the gold. This time I descended and ascended like an experienced diver, and the crew hauled me on deck to wait for the blast below.

Well, the blast went off successfully, but like Horatio Swanfire had learned millennia before, sometimes the most carefully laid plans can go terribly wrong. In our case, 'twasn't the fact that we used inferior explosives—nay! Seems we used too powerful a charge! For the explosion ripped open the seafloor straight down to the molten core of the earth, sucking the gold with it and creating a great whirlpool that threatened to drain the Gulf of Mexico bone dry!

You ever watch the water in a bathtub circle around the drain? Well, imagine the water circling like that a hundred yards across, and the ship you're on circling the whirlpool faster and faster—that's the precise predicament in which we found ourselves that day!

The crew, sensing imminent disaster upon us—yea, upon the entire world—jumped ship just as fast they could. I grabbed my trusty bucket and did the same. In fact, all of us jumped ship, save for the Captain who had the worst case of gold fever possible. He knew what lay beneath the sea and reckoned it to be the only thing in the world that mattered. But that fever would cost him dearly, children—yea, his very life!

As the ship rounded the whirlpool in ever tightening circles—its deck boards splintering in the air—Captain Humdinger clung to the helm and bellowed into the abyss:

"Give me treasure or give me death!"

As he spoke, so it was. The whirlpool sucked Captain Humdinger and his vessel into the ocean below, and that three-masted ship, being a goodly size, did plug the hole in the bottom of the Gulf to prevent the draining of those 660 quadrillion gallons of water.

'Tis a sad story, children—a sad story indeed. But the events of that day taught me a thing or two about being satisfied with what I have, and I pray you understand that better after hearing of my travails on the Gulf of Mexico.

Now, getting down to brass tacks, the moral of this story, the very crux of it, is that when you focus on God, you don't have to worry. Or, as we like to say in the mining camp, *"I have learned the secret to being content no matter the grade of the ore. I am content whether the yield is rich or scarce. I am content whether I have lack or plenty."*

Which means, dear children, if you have a warm, dry place to lay your head tonight and your stomach ain't crying out to you in pangs of hunger—rejoice! God has given you plenty!

And if you long for things you just don't have, remember, too, that God is watching over you, and knows exactly what you need to thrive in this world. Rejoice in that too, for it will comfort you and make you wise—wise enough to face any challenge this fallen world may toss your way.

5 A SWASHBUCKLER'S TALE (1834)

"I regarded the enemy not lightly, as I squared-off against the first bouncing, drooling seven-footer to invade the camp."

I n times past, as anyone acquainted with my history (either by direct knowledge, or reading prior entries in this journal) will attest, I traveled far and wide, scouring vast territories in the farthest reaches of the globe in search of my fortune and destiny.

Round about the age of 17, that is, in the year 1834, the same year I married my lovely bride Millicent (but before our darling daughter Clementine sprang to life,) it so happened that I found myself indebted to an investor, of sorts, who had lent me money to purchase shovels, pick axes, a worthy donkey, and mining rights to land that never quite panned out. Now, this investor, being a hard man, but being a fair man, too, conceived of a way for me to make good on my debts while helping him further along his investment schemes.

This investor and treasure-seeker, going by the name of Percival Gottlieb, asked for my help to establish a mining camp on the other side of the world. He promised the quest would not be easy, nor was it likely to be rewarding for me beyond satisfying my debts, nor did he suspect I would survive, but he said he had a gut feeling I was the kind of young man who would only reach his highest potential by rising to a great challenge.

Furthermore, Percival said, should I grant him two years of my life in such a venture, why, he promised to cancel my debt and repay me the same amount in wages, plus a small percentage of the output of the mine. And so I, being young, naïve and a wee-bit puffed up by the sliver of flattery that had gotten under my skin, agreed to throw my lot into his boneheaded scheme.

Now, Percival—or Percy to those he counted worthy to call him such—had laid claim to several hectares of wilderness in the valleys of colonial Victoria (Australia, that is), which he reckoned ought to contain vast deposits of gold, the likes of which men could only dream. How he came to such a conclusion remains a mystery to this day, although it was said he had a nose for that sort of thing—yea, even if the scent be half way around the world!

I set out with old Percy Gottlieb aboard a cargo vessel bound for the land down under. After stops in Rio de Janeiro, Brazil and Cape Town, South Africa—where many remarkable events occurred which shall not be recounted at this time—we arrived in Australia to find a land of greater hardships than we ever imagined. Yea, the day we disembarked, we doubted our dreams of destiny and fortune more than at any time during our seven months of squalor upon the open sea!

Nonetheless, Percy and I set about the business of establishing a mining camp in the outback. We secured supplies as they could be had from cargo ships coming into port, and hired several able-bodied Aboriginals—that is, descendants of folks living in Australia before the Europeans arrived—to blast and dig and process ore out of the hills that Percy felt certain would, any day now, reveal evidence that his hectares encompassed the Motherlode of all gold deposits in the world.

But that first year proved to be more desolate and less fortuitous than even our first inklings suggested straight off the boat. Yea, June and July (that being wintertime, down under) brought near freezing temperatures, weather for which we were not rightly prepared. And given the scarcity of food, why, we succumbed to boiling and eating shoe leather just to survive!

The cold weather didn't let up none in the springtime, either. The meager crops we planted to supplement the food supplies trickling in from port never quite took off. Oh, dear children, I laid down to bed most nights with sharp hunger pangs in my belly, wondering if I'd live to see another sunrise. And if you think that was unfortunate, I should point out that the few of us there in the mining camp weren't the only creatures besieged by cruel hunger—no! It seems the grasses and brush on the plains did not grow quite the way they had in times gone by, and so that year the kangaroos that roamed wild in those parts grew hungry, gaunt and hideous, with darkened, sunken eye sockets and foam bubbling from the corners of their mouths.

Why, they looked like hairy skeletons hopping around the outskirts of the camp. Indeed, as we lay down to sleep at night, with the sound of our bellies rumbling like distant thunder, just below that sound we could hear the kangaroos, gnawing on our fence posts, threatening to eat away our camp as we slept. Old Percy, in fact, suspected the beasts were not only mad with hunger, but stricken with rabies, too, and reckoned it was only a matter of time before they breached our camp and devoured us in our sleep!

Under these stark conditions, we were grateful—nay, overjoyed—to receive a delivery of food rations from the port. The stale crusts of bread, a few cans of peanut butter and several hands of mushy brown bananas weren't exactly fit for human consumption, but we looked upon them with hungry eyes. Seeing that this food was the only thing separating us from a future life on this earth and the great hereafter up above, we divvied up the rations among the men and kept them on our persons at all times.

I, for one, made several peanut butter and banana sandwiches and tucked these in my waistband for safe keeping. But as we luxuriated in our newfound provisions, the kangaroos encroached upon our camp with greater frequency and a heretofore unglimpsed ferocity, shaking the fences at dusk like a mighty storm blowing across the plains.

And so it was we established a rotating shift of watchmen, and built a guard tower enshrining an iron bell, with tiki torches all about the perimeter of the camp, so that if the unthinkable happened—that is, should the rabid, starving kangaroos break through the fence in the dead of night—we'd be prepared to meet our glory or demise with our half-eaten boots on!

Well, as destiny or fate, blind chance or rotten luck, or God's divine plan had it—I'll let you be the judge (I have my own understanding of these events)—the kangaroos breached the fence on my watch, causing me to raise the alarm bell and leap from the guard tower, fists to the fore.

Now, I reckon most of you children don't realize that kangaroos are excellent boxers, having not only stood toe-to-toe with many skilled human pugilists throughout history, but prevailed upon them as well!

Thus, I regarded the enemy not lightly as I squared-off against the first bouncing, drooling seven-footer to invade the camp. I jabbed and hooked, throwing a series of deft combinations that found their mark, rattling the great marsupial. He shook off the blows, grabbed me by the ears and kicked me in the gut until I lost my air, and then my consciousness. Oh, I dare say I believed that was my last stand! But then, the blackness that had overtaken me gave way to a pale morning light, with smoldering tiki torches bleeding off tendrils of smoke, and the voices of my fellow miners warbling a victory cheer.

As Percy later told me, the ringing of the iron bell roused the miners from their slumber, allowing them just enough time to cast nets over the horde of kangaroos; once netted, the men shut them inside crates, which we took by wagon into port and sent them on a one-way trip to Tasmania.

Now, if that was the end of the story, why, it wouldn't be much of a story at all, seeing that I fought a hungry animal and lost badly. But as it happened, the next day, as I ventured outside of the camp and into the wilderness, basking in rare sunshine that pierced the clouds that spring afternoon, I came upon a joey, hobbled in one leg and stuck in a thicket.

Even though a rabid marsupial had nearly killed me the day before, I harbored no malice toward the joey—no! I felt only an overwhelming sense of pity, which led me to free the poor creature from what ensnared him. And I should tell you he let out a little yelp, frightened, alone, not knowing that his kinfolk was crated off and transported to Tasmania.

As strange as it may sound to you—although it makes perfect sense to me to this day—I straightaway thought of that man Mephibosheth from the Bible, the son of Jonathan and grandson of King Saul, who relied on the mercy and grace of David to shield him from harm. Over the course of the next year, I nursed the joey back to strength, building him a pogo-crutch he could fit under his arm to hop around on, dividing my rations of peanut butter and banana sandwiches with him until he put on a little weight. Why, that joey even learned the ropes around the camp, so that once his leg healed and he abandoned the pogo-crutch, he could push a wheel barrow full of ore to the processing pile twice as fast as the fastest miner!

With that, I knew my destiny and fortune in the land down under had been found, and I collected my wages from Percival Gottlieb. Subsequently, Joey and I set off for port, where I purchased us tickets to Tasmania. Oh, dear children, you should have seen the joy in the hops of those kangaroos when Joey was at last reunited with his kinfolk. 'Twas the kind of treasure you can't find buried in stone—no! That kind of treasure is only found right here, inside the heart.

As for me, I set sail from Tasmania to my own homeland, these United States of America, where I knew my own kinfolk waited to be found, and greater adventures were yet to be had!

So, getting down to brass tacks, the moral of this story, the very crux of it, is that we should treat others the way we want them to treat us. Or, as we said in that mining camp down under, *"Do unto the kangaroos as you would have them do unto you."* This saying is a variation on a teaching from the Good Book itself, which, being of such great value, is known as the Golden Rule. And as you know, dear children, I have a warm place in my heart for all things gold, but this nugget of truth trumps them all.

6 INTO THE VOLCANO (1847)

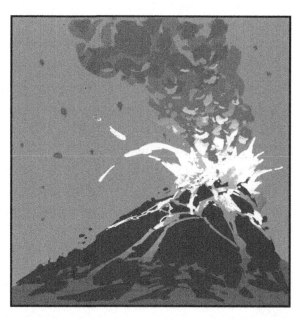

"Standing before the stone altar, at the edge of the lava pool, the henchmen of Moctezuma placed the tips of their spears into the smalls of our backs..."

I n the autumn of 1847, a little after harvest time had come and gone, Millicent, Clementine and I had just stumbled upon information from a trusted source regarding the location of the lost San Saba mine, said to contain enough gold and silver to avail a young man of all his earthly desires until his sunset years, with plenty left in reserve for a mighty inheritance to his children and grandchildren!

That being the case, we camped in east Texas at the intersection of two prominent trading routes in order to amass much needed supplies for our treasure hunt, and to secure some well-deserved rest and relaxation after being on the move for the better part of a year.

But twasn't long before several merchants working the trading routes, merchants from the deep interior of Mexico, arrived with tales of a great volcano they said was a billowing smoke, strong and tall up into the clouds—straight and true like a great tower, unaffected by the swirling winds—which was a sure sign it was fixing to blow its top!

Now, as any miner worth his salt will tell you, gold pools in abundance around areas of volcanic activity, mainly because of all the lava being forced to the surface, which produces metal-rich rock. This metal-rich rock, in turn, settles into caverns and the surrounding river banks, meaning a single good blast from the volcano might very well unload tons of gold on the surface within easy reach of anyone who knows where to look.

Armed with this knowledge, we set aside our quest for the Lost San Saba mine until another day, reasoning the imminent eruption of the Mexican volcano was the more promising of the two ventures. And twasn't many weeks afterward we found ourselves on the outskirts of Mexico City, viewing the pillar of smoke rising from the volcano with our own eyes.

We hired a guide—a man by the name of Don Miguel—well-acquainted with the caves and rivers around the volcano, to lead us to promising points to mine and pan for gold, to translate for us into the tongue of the natives and to secure fresh water and food along the way. Don Miguel brought with him his darling daughter Maria, who was with child, and her groom José.

As we traveled toward the grumbling volcano, Don Miguel shared how the land of Mexico City was settled. You see, when the Aztecs first arrived to the valley, they wandered about for a considerable number of days before settling down at a place where they observed an eagle perched upon a cactus and feasting upon a serpent. They took this for a sign their god had granted them rest in the land.

The volcano rising out of the valley, which they named Popocatepetl—but I can't say the name too well, so I just call it The Big Cat—meant in their own language 'smoking mountain.' Don Miguel told us in gruesome detail how the Aztecs made human sacrifices on the mountain slopes to appease their god. Truth be told, they worshiped over a thousand false gods, and they seemed to have one for everything you can imagine—gods of beauty, gods of rain, gods of the wind and even gods of flowers. But the god to whom they made human sacrifices was the most wicked of them all, and he was the god of the sun and of war. His name was Huitzilopochtli—but I have trouble saying his name, too, so I'll just call him Hootsie.

Now, as we made our way through the valley that lay at the foot of the great smoldering volcano, we were attacked by a tribe of angry Aztecs living nearby, who believed the grumblings of The Big Cat were a sign that Hootsie was angry about one thing or another. Seeing us, the idea alighted upon the Aztec high priest that Hootsie was angry about foreigners being in the land. The only remedy, he reasoned, was for one of us foreigners to be put to death!

Yea, this high priest, who went by the name of Moctezuma, did decree to Don Miguel that none other than the virginal Clementine should be offered as a sacrifice to the false and wicked god.

Oh, dear children, I don't mind telling you I was a shaking in fear something awful as the Aztecs led us up the volcano, to a stone altar they had erected on the edge of a lava pool. I can't rightly say whether 'twas the volcano shaking beneath my feet, or my knees knocking together, but so bad was the shaking that my eyebrows and mustache darn near fell off my face!

And the worst part of the ordeal was that Moctezuma declared I must be the one to sacrifice Clem there on the altar, with an obsidian knife he had fashioned out of the volcanic rock. Standing before the stone altar, at the edge of the lava pool, the henchmen of Moctezuma placed the tips of their spears into the smalls of our backs, threatening to drive us into the swirling lava of the volcano should we object to the high priest's demands. Now, I was of the mind to let them drive me into the volcano—and so was Millicent—for it seemed they aimed to cut down Clementine one way or another. But far be it from us that we should be active participants in such a gory display of obeisance to their false god. No!

But it was Clem herself who turned to me, with a faint, resolved smile on her face and a calm and settled demeanor about her whole personage, reminding me of many passages from the Good Book that weren't rightly on my mind at the moment. For starters, she compared herself to Esther, asking me, as Esther's close family member Mordecai did, if perhaps she had been brought into existence for such a time as this?

Then, she reminded me of Hannaniah, Mishael and Azariah (known to history by their Babylonian names Shadrach, Meshach and Abednego), and how they withstood

King Nebuchadnezzar, when he threatened to throw them into the fiery furnace if they did not worship his graven image, declaring that, and I quote, "If this be so, our God whom we serve is able to deliver us from the burning fiery furnace, and he will deliver us out of your hand, O king. But if not, be it known to you, O king, that we will not serve your gods or worship the golden image that you have set up."

And she reminded me of the prophet Elijah contending with the priests of Baal, and of David withstanding the giant Goliath to his face, and of the Apostle Peter being crucified upside down for refusing to deny Jesus before godless men. She reminded me of their obedience to the One who sits in judgment over this entire world.

Finally, she reminded me of the time when the Lord commanded Abraham to take his only begotten son of Sarah—Isaac, the son of promise—to a place he would show him and sacrifice him there. Abraham, having come of age in a pagan culture where human sacrifice was a matter of course, much like the present land of Mexico in which we found ourselves, did obey the Lord in binding his son of promise on the altar and raising up the blade against him, reasoning in his mind that since God had promised the descendants of Isaac would number more than the stars in the sky or the sand on the seashore, that even should he lower the blade upon his son, why, the Lord would bring him back to life in order to fulfill His promise!

Well, I tell you the solid gold truth, dear children, I could not have been more proud of my Clementine in that moment, for she displayed all the godliness of the martyr Stephen in her recitations of the Scriptures! Her faith gave me strength, which begat hope, and further bred certainty that in all things that were to follow, the Lord God Almighty would be revealed and set on high.

With Clementine's assurances, I turned to the high priest and asked for the obsidian blade which they had prepared for the sacrifice. Taking the dagger, I paraphrased the words of Hannaniah, Mishael and Azariah, saying, "O Moctezuma, the God whom we serve is able to deliver Clementine from the point and edge of this blade—yea, even the belly of this great volcano—and He will do it before your very eyes! But even if He chooses not to, be it known we will never serve your god—and furthermore, we think your god is a bit of a cry baby!"

Moctezuma flushed in the cheeks as if no one had ever spoken to him so forthrightly in all his years. Knowing not what else to do, he genuflected before the lava pool, perhaps in prayer to Hootsie.

After a long moment, Moctezuma arose from his kneeling position and faced us. He affirmed that Hootsie demanded an outsider must be put to death to appease him—no bones about it—and so I must raise the obsidian blade and strike down Clementine. However, if the Lord of whom I spoke instead provided a ransom, in exchange for Clementine, why, then we would all go free.

At this point, a procession of Aztec women arrived with baskets of flower petals, with which they covered the altar thick, like a mattress. On top of the altar, they bound Clementine with heavy cords.

Trusting in God Almighty for deliverance, I did raise the obsidian knife to sacrifice my darling daughter Clementine, just as Moctezuma demanded. But, dear children, I'm here to tell you at that precise moment the most remarkable turn of events occurred that cannot be explained be anything less than divine intervention—which is a fancy way of saying God came to the rescue!

For you see, no sooner did I raise the obsidian blade than we all heard the screech of an eagle—the most sacred bird to the Aztec people. Looking up, we beheld that mighty bird swooping down from the sky with a snake in its mouth, and as it soared above the lava pool, the eagle dropped the serpent into the fiery lava of The Big Cat! What's more, the smoke billowing from the mountain vanished, and all traces of quaking ceased!

Well, dear children, given the fact that the appearance of the eagle with a serpent in its mouth did so neatly mirror the legend of how the Aztecs first came to settle the valley, and the subsequent stilling of the volcano, it should come as no surprise that Moctezuma and all the Aztecs fell awestruck on their faces.

Don Miguel urged us to seize the moment and run for our lives, but I knew God had not spared us to flee. For you see, the ransoming of Clementine gave me an opportunity to share with Moctezuma of a time when fiery serpents beset the children of Israel in the wilderness, and Moses lifted up a serpent on a staff that whosoever looked at it should be healed of their bites. Further, I told of how Jesus Himself said that just as Moses lifted up the serpent in the wilderness, even so the Son of Man need be lifted up. I explained how the sacrifice of Christ occurred once for all time, and that no other sacrifice was required of men—no! Indeed, no sacrifice performed a thousand times over—yea, some thousand-thousand times, could ever do.

Moctezuma heard the Gospel and wept. Then, through his tears, he explained to us how the flowers the women brought to the sacrifice were known as *mirasols*, said to be the favorite flower of Hootsie. Moctezuma thought it of great interest that the name mirasol, when translated into English, meant to 'look at the sun.' He said from then on the flowers would not remind him to look at the sun, that is, the great ball of fire in the sky, but to 'look at the Son,' the Son of God.

In the days to follow, Moctezuma tore down the altar to the false and wicked god Hootsie and plunged it into the lava pool. In its place, he planted a garden of mirasols—a reminder that Jesus alone is the sacrifice, light and life of the world, to as many as will believe. Moctezuma, finding hope, delight and the means of salvation in the Gospel, did commit himself and his household—yea, the entire tribe that followed him—to our Lord and Savior Jesus Christ.

And from the moment the eagle dropped the serpent into the volcano, the rumbling and smoldering ceased for a period of many years. With no imminent eruption in sight, and therefore no fashioning of gold from the great furnace of the volcano, we bid our hosts farewell, heading north, back into the land of Texas where rumor had it, a gold and silver mine of great value, known as the San Saba mine, lay lost to history and waiting to be found!

So, getting down to brass tacks, the moral of this story, the very crux of it, is that we should lean on God, trusting not in our own understanding, because He has something much bigger in mind than we can imagine. Or, as the Good Book puts it, in Psalms 61:2, *"Lead me to the Rock that is higher than I."*

7 THE CHRISTMAS MIRACLE OF 1847

"An ethereal light enveloped the plains, the snows drifting from linen-white to rainbow waves, and the lot of us turned our gazes upward to see a sight I had no mind to imagine in a Texas sky."

Here we are, children, smack dab in the midst of the Christmas season, and what a glorious time that is to be alive! Foremost, 'tis a time when we can set aside our cares of the year and reflect on the greatest gift the world has ever known—yea, I mean the birth of our Lord and Savior Jesus Christ! But not only that, 'tis an occasion to look ahead and wonder upon the promise of a brand-new year.

But for me, dear children—well, I've lived a long life and encountered a sluice full of hardship and bliss, and the story I'm fixing to share with you today concerns a miracle I witnessed on Christmas Day, way back in the year of 1847! Now, the events leading up to the miracle—and those that took place just after—are what resonate in my soul whenever I hear the word Christmas. Yes, indeed—'tis the reason Christmas is a bittersweet season for me.

Now, you children understand I am known as the Miner 49er, and for good reason; I helped blaze that trail across the countryside to California during the great Gold Rush of 1849. But truth be told, I was a searching for my fortune long before then. Indeed, gold fever is what brought me, my lovely bride Millicent, and our darling daughter Clementine to the nation of Mexico and the former Republic of Texas that winter of 1847.

The history of how we ended up in Mexico and the slew of curious incidents that transpired there must wait for another day, but 'tis enough to say our retreat from Mexico led us into Texas on a quest for the Lost San Saba Mine, which we believed, if found, would bring us glory, long length of life, and wealth beyond all our wildest imaginations!

Joining us on our trek were a handful of new fortune-seekers, including a young man named José, and his tender bride Maria, who was far along with child at the time. Indeed, the doctor who traveled with us said she might give birth at any time—yea, like a clap of thunder waking you from a dream.

As we forged north that December, deeper and deeper into Texas—our sights set on untangling the mystery of the Lost San Saba Mine—there were no blue skies of which to speak, neither in fact nor metaphor. No! For you see, winter arrived harshly to the wilderness of Texas, with cold days and colder nights, torrential rainstorms and stiff, buffeting winds to slow our progress. This turn in the weather affected Millicent more than the rest of us, starting with the sniffles and a mild cough, but soon evolved into lethargy, dark circles under her eyes and a rasping in the depths of her lungs.

And, as I mentioned before, young Maria, being so far along with child, labored to travel at the hearty clip we'd become accustomed to in the summer months, even riding upon the back of a mule. Our pace slowed to a slither, and we soon whittled our rations to a pittance per day. We found ourselves in dire circumstances that Christmas Eve—cold, hungry and grateful to God just to be alive. Now, do any of you children know what the phrase dire circumstances means? Well, it indicates trouble, disaster, misfortune and the like—but hardly yet did we know the meaning of that phrase—not with the dreadful turn of events about to befall our haggard band of fortune-seekers.

When we set out that Christmas Eve morning from our makeshift camp, the rains came heavy and the temperature dropped to the freezing point. Every hair on my head spoke of coming snows—yea, my eyebrows, mustache, and chin whiskers stiffened up like the hairs on a wild boar, which is a far better forecaster than any weatherman! And to throw gunpowder on the fire, around noontime Maria complained of terrible pains in her belly—which the doctor assured us meant the birth of the bebé (that's the Spanish word for baby,) was well-nigh.

To say we were ill-prepared for such a turn of events would be an understatement, since none of us had seen snow in many years. In the case of José and Maria, why, they'd never laid eyes on that intricately branched, hexagonal form of agglomerated ice crystals known as snowflakes. No! In fact, when the rains changed over to fat, heavy snowflakes, falling the size of silver dollars—the delicate, labor-pained Maria, perched on the mule and wrapped in triple ponchos to protect her from the cold, kept muttering a single phrase, over and over again: *I'll go down, I'll go down, I'll go down.*

Well, my bride Millicent knew all about the pangs of childbirth—seeing that Clementine was a lively child—and she urged José and the doctor to help Maria off the mule. She told them straight to their faces, "Have some common sense, gentlemen, and listen to the young girl. She says she wants down!"

The doctor let out a long peal of laughter, tumbling headfirst into a snowbank. As you might imagine, what with Millicent being as headstrong as she was, this peeved her to no end—even in the throes of her sickness—and when the doctor stood up, she scooped a handful of snow, pressed it into a hard, little ball and fired it at him with the aim of Annie Oakley, striking him square behind the ear and laying him flat on his keister.

Now, it took the doctor a moment to recover his senses. Once he did, he remonstrated, "You don't understand. She's not saying, 'I'll go down.' She's saying, *algodon*—in Spanish that means cotton. She thinks the sky is blowing cotton!"

Well, this caused Millicent no small amount of embarrassment. We all shared a long laugh at this, falling over ourselves, rolling around in the snow till our bellies hurt and we were sopping wet from crown to heel. Yes, indeed! It was just the levity needed to break us free from the icy hands of doom we'd wrapped ourselves in and lift our spirits high enough to take action.

For you see, children, a wilderness beset by a snowstorm is no reasonable place for a woman to bear a child. And yet, we had little reason to expect any other fate for Maria and her blessed bebé. Our best prospect was to seek shelter, pray that Maria's labor pains subsided and outlast the Christmas Eve storm. And so we forged ahead. In a few miles, we came upon a pass that snaked between two rocky buttes, cut there, no doubt, by the Great Flood of old.

As we entered the gap, so began a series of events best described—even by the most hard-boiled of skeptics—as divine intervention. Now, do you children know what divine intervention is? Why, it's nothing less than God taking an active role in the affairs of men, which is another way of saying we were about to experience some miracles! Yea, the first of those miracles was the sound of birdsong echoing over the walls of the buttes, which led us—as the Good Lord saw fit—to a cave to shelter in for the night.

Oh, let me tell you, children—that cave could have been a mansion fit for John Jacob Astor himself, for it granted us respite from the driving snows and howling winds. We gathered enough straw, tumbleweeds and deadwood in that pass to allow us the luxury of feeding the horses and the mule, fixing some proper bedding for Maria, and building us a camp fire to dry our clothes and restore some manner of warmth to our gelid bones. All the while we sheltered in the cave, we heard the birdsong, just as if we were lazing out in the middle of a field in springtime.

But even with our spirits lifted, having secured shelter full of melodious birdsong, and reflecting on the plastering of the good doctor with a snowball behind the ear, we had to face the grim reality that we were socked inside of a cave, miles from only God knew where, with a woman on the cusp of childbirth!

Twasn't long before—as we sat inside that cave huddled around the crackling fire—that we watched the snow amass, first a foot high, then two, then as deep as a man's fastened belt buckle. The doctor, who'd been checking on Maria as the snow accumulated, paced back and forth before the fire.

"Doc, what's got you in a tither?" I sensed something weighed heavy on his heart, for he had the look of a man haunted by dark visions of things to come. At that point, the doctor ceased his pacing and removed his glasses, rubbing the lenses clean on the tail of his shirt.

He said, in a quiet voice so as not to alarm the others, "The little bebé is breach. Old Maria will need more care than I can rightly offer."

Now, if you children don't know what breach means, don't worry none about that—'tis enough to say it ain't no easy way for a baby to be born. But more significant in the doctor's statement was that he'd called young Maria *Old Maria*—and people don't go around calling somebody old unless they perceive that person ain't got much time left in the world.

I understood this, and from the look José cast my way, I knew he understood it too. And so the both of us, understanding what we understood, stepped outside the cave into the waist high snow for a private conversation.

We could see plainly that someone must hike out of the pass and locate, as fast as possible, some outpost of civilization where we could summon the help the good doctor required. But we could also see the horses were of no use to us, what with the depth of the snow, and that such an undertaking might be a fool's errand. Nevertheless, we determined 'twas better to be fools than second guessers.

José and I gathered up supplies—some rope, four flatter pieces of deadwood to tie beneath our shoes, two fingers worth of beef jerky, and then we set to breaking loose the travel-trunk lids to use as wedges against the wall of snow. Now, it was at this point that Millicent came out of the cave to see what all the ruckus was about.

I thought she'd be proud of us and our noble undertaking, but no! When she understood that I aimed to take José away from Maria at this precious crossroads in their lives—yea, the birth of their first child—why, she refused to let it be.

"José will stay here," she said, "and I'll set off for civilization with you."

Oh, how I wanted to reason her out of that decision, realizing her cough weren't getting no better—might be the onset of pneumonia, for all I knew—but when Millicent decided on a thing, why, she became immovable as a chain of mountains. So, with no way around the matter, we bade Clementine and the others farewell, uncertain if we'd ever see them again.

As we left the pass between the buttes, out onto the open plains, several events transpired that one cannot rightly explain by coincidence, happenstance, or fortune alone. Yea! If one has eyes to see, why, he can only see the unfolding of more miracles. For the wind-driven snow stopped within the single beat of a heart, the clouds above rolled away like a scroll, and sweet sainted starlight shone down to guide us on our way.

The second event which came on the tail of the first— and yea, more miraculous than the first—was the sound of birdsong behind us. As we turned to see whence it came, our eyes lit upon the unbelievable sight of five golden finches flying at us out of the night and settling down on the brims of our oilskin hats!

We took this for a good omen, continuing our press through the snows while singing our favorite Christmas songs. But then, slicing through our cheerful melody was a sound that—if I didn't know no better—was the siren song of teenage girls throwing a slumber party. But teenage girls don't throw slumber parties on the December snow-swept plains of Texas. Which meant it could be only one thing: a pack of coyotes!

Well, if you never heard such a soul-piercing noise in your lives, thank your lucky stars! 'Tis a sound that'll send chills over your whole body, tie up your innards in knots no sailor can undo, and cause your toe-hairs to stand straight up on end! But the acoustics of the snow-blanketed plains left us unable to figure the exact direction whence the whelp of the coyotes came, so we thought it best to press on the way we was going.

This decision, children, would've proved to be an error of the highest magnitude, were it not for yet another miracle to confront us on our way. For no sooner had we crested the next rise than we stood face to face with a pack of nine—count 'em, nine!—coyotes, looking about as lean and mean and ravenous as any creatures you ever laid eyes upon. But then, an ethereal light enveloped the plains, the snows drifting from linen-white into rainbow waves, and the lot of us—and I do mean those coyotes, too—lifted our eyes to see a sight I had no mind to imagine in a Texas sky. Lo-and-behold, as we gazed heavenward, it appeared a multitude of angels stood among the constellations of the sky, gazing down at us.

Now, my first thought was the thought of a man. I thought that what my eyes were laying witness to was nothing more than the Aurora Borealis creating brilliant streaks and swaths and pillars of color up there in the sky. But, for it to be the Aurora Borealis, so far south as the heartland of Texas— why, 'twould entail a solar phenomenon of the rarest and most spectacular kind—yea, a kind seen only once every four or five generations.

Even so, that explanation held no water with me when I conceived it. For as soon as those pillars of light appeared in the sky, those salivating coyotes, who only seconds before had eyed Millicent and me as their next dinner, hunkered in the snow with tails curled around their haunches, ears pressed flat against their heads. Yea, it seemed like an intelligence had becalmed those wild beasts.

At this point—strange as it were—those five golden finches nestled on our hats took flight, bobbing and weaving in front of the snouts of the coyotes. Each time they did, it broke the transfixion of the dogs, causing them to lurch forward and snap at the birds, trying their utmost to snatch 'em out of the air.

This odd behavior by the coyotes gave me an idea. Now, even though they scared me something fierce, you children know a thing or two about my exploits in days gone by—the way I wrestled with sharks and gators, and once, in my younger days, how I fist-fought a rabid kangaroo on the outback of Australia (I didn't win that one; why, he just about drummed me off the continent) but the point is, I always enjoyed a challenge. So, with the unfurled rope, I harnessed and lashed together the coyotes, while Millicent affixed the hoods of the travel-trunks to the ropes. Just like that, we had us a dogsled team like they run up yonder in the Yukon.

We traveled by our coyote-sled on into Christmas morning, until we reached a trading village where we corralled us a posse of able-bodied men, a midwife and enough supplies to see us through to the New Year.

Better yet, the sun came out that morning, and the temperature rose, causing a melt-off of the snow, allowing us to set the coyotes free and take up a stagecoach back to the cave between the buttes. You'd think this was the most glorious morning of our imaginations—and 'twould've been, but for the fact that Millicent's cough turned for the worse. She lay in my arms close to death the whole ride back to the buttes. Once there, we reclined her on a bed of tumbleweeds and ponchos and prayed for one more miracle.

But, children, even at your young age, I hope you understand that God is not a magician, or a genie in a bottle from whom we demand wishes. No! He is the Sovereign Lord of this universe Who understands things we can't even begin to wrap our feeble minds around. While He always hears our prayers, sometimes the answer is no. Sometimes, He has in mind a far better future than the thing for which we pray.

So it was that Christmas Day of 1847. As I held onto Millicent's hand, she passed from this world to the next. That same day, however, the good doctor and the midwife delivered a healthy baby girl into the arms of her mammy Maria. Believe you me, you ain't seen joy until you seen the joy brought about by a little bebé welcomed into this world— doubly so for José and Maria as they reflected on the events that preceded that Christmas morn.

Maria, awestruck as she was that Millicent had undertaken the saintly duty to find help in that time of need— yea, had yielded her very life so the bebé might be delivered safely into Maria's arms—named the child Millicent, which, in the French tongue, doth mean 'of a thousand saints,' for she felt so many self-sacrificing individuals surrounded her that day.

Now, I'd be remiss if I didn't tell you how this story ended that Christmas long ago. For you see, while much celebration followed the birth of the bebé Millicent, we could not neglect laying to rest my own Millicent by sunset. And so, Clementine told her farewells to her mother there in the cave, and then I knelt to hold the hands of my departed bride one last time. As I reflected on our lives together, weeping for the loss of one so dear, I happened to look up at the cavern walls. There, in the flickering campfire light, I read two words scrawled on the rock: San Saba. Indeed, for all our calculated searching, we had sheltered by happenstance in the very mine for which we'd sacrificed so much.

But the funny thing is, children, nobody that day spoke of gold or silver or diamonds—nay, no material possessions whatsoever. We sang praises to God, and thanked Him for that original Christmas of old, when He sent His one and only Son into this world to die for our sins. And so it seemed good to me to pick up a stone, and with a strong and steady hand obliterate those words "San Saba" from the wall of the cave. For you see, dear children, the true treasure of San Saba was what my lovely bride Millicent had given up so that José and Maria might have a future and a hope. I determined the cave would be her final resting place—never to be blasted or mined for something as fleeting as gold.

So, getting down to brass tacks, the moral of this story, the very crux of it and the true meaning of Christmas, is that in this world we ought to give much, because we have received much. Or, as the Good Book so records in Isaiah 7:14,

"Therefore, the Lord Himself shall give you a sign: Behold, a virgin shall conceive, and bear a Son, and shall call His name Immanuel.

8 THE PURSE OF EARRINGS (1848)

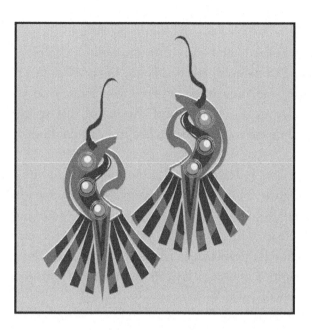

"The bandit was no amateur, whipping one revolver after another from his saddlebag, draining the cylinders in a strobing, crackling cloud of gunsmoke, until only the whinnies of a few horses drifted up from the gully below."

Children, even at your tender ages I'm certain you already know that treasures come in all shapes and sizes—a fortune of Texas cotton, for instance, would fill the hull of an ocean-steady ship, while a fortune in diamonds, such as the Rock-like-no-other that Tea Leaves and I discovered, why, that sort of treasure fits squarely in the palm of a 49er.

I bring this up for point of comparison. The last time we were together, I told you about my quest for the Lost San Saba Mine, which you could no more fit into the palm of the hand than you could cram into the hull of a ship! Now, the treasure I'm fixing to tell you about today rivals in value all of San Saba and then some, and yet you wear it on the body. Yea, I do mean jewelry—and the lot of this jewelry, when gathered together, could be tucked into the confines of a lady's purse.

Now, following the death of my saintly bride Millicent in that great Christmas blizzard of 1847, Clementine and I separated from our fellow treasure-seekers. José and Maria, with their sparkling new bebé, were eager to return to the land of their forefathers, back in Mexico. Clem and I, though, were as determined as ever to lay our hands on our fortune awaiting us in the wild, wild West!

You see, we heard rumblings of legends that the early Spanish explorers in those parts, known to history as the Conquistadors, had once upon a time discovered a land called Cibola, home to Seven Cities of Gold! But, before they returned word of their discovery to the Spanish throne, their once trusty guide—a Moroccan by the name of Estabanico—forsook them. Estabanico, finding in Cibola all he had ever desired from life, refused to leave. So, the Spaniards set out alone, got all turned around in the wilderness, and by the time they reached base camp three months later—hungry, sunburnt, and blistered—why, they had no clear recollection of how to return to that city of incomparable wealth!

To be sure, the Conquistadors dispatched several search parties in the following years to locate Cibola, but 'twas all for naught. With each party that returned disillusioned and empty-handed, the Seven Cities of Gold became less of a historical fact and more the stuff of legend. But for those of us who believed, why, we continued to persevere, hoping one day we would walk those streets paved with gold.

So it was in the springtime of that year, as I followed the clues I'd gathered, with my darling Clementine at my side, and our fearless donkey Clip-Clop hauling our supplies, that we traveled about three days yonder to the west through the disputed territories between Mexico and Texas, along a little worn wagon trail, when we encountered a situation a person rightly don't ever want to encounter.

I was leading Clip-Clop by the reins, with Clementine lagging behind—she was picking wildflowers trail side—when we crested the top of a butte that led into a gully below. From our vantage, we saw a stagecoach of exquisite design, emblazoned on the side with the seal of the Mexican government. Now, if you haven't seen the seal before, why, it depicts an eagle with a snake in its mouth. As for the stagecoach, it was barred from going no further by a massive pile of dead trees, branches and dry hay piled as high as Goliath.

An entourage of a hundred military men in full uniform surrounded the stagecoach. Some rode horseback, most went by foot—but all traveled armed to the teeth with bayonet-fitted muskets. The Captain of the company appeared a measure perplexed by their current situation, inspecting the dead trees and branches and hay blocking the trail, when a young-looking man—yea, he had the face of a baby—emerged from beyond the gully on horseback. He rode up to the Captain and dismounted his steed. The two men commiserated about their predicament—that is to say, no one's feathers got plucked in the exchange. Then, the lone rider offered the Captain a cigar from the pocket of his vest, lighted it for him and carelessly tossed the match into the pile of dead wood and hay. The entire mass burst into sky high flames!

Well, it goes without saying that this got the Captain shouting loud enough for Clem and I to hear, and I will say those weren't no kind words foaming from his mouth. Nay, I covered Clementine's delicate ears for fear she might faint. Well, the baby-faced rider made a series of apologetic bows as he backed away from the conflagration and the Captain marshaled his platoons to bring their botas forward—that is, their canteens of water—to douse the flames.

This seemed to be a careless act by a bumbling young fool; that is, until that baby-faced rider strolled to a different pile of hay, some twenty yards off the trail. He swiped his foot across the top of it, revealing a wooden box with a long handle. For the life of me, it looked like a dynamite detonator, and events would soon prove my surmise correct. He plunged the handle, sparking a current of electricity through a wire buried along the trail, spitting sand and puffs of dust all the way back to the mouth of the gully flanked by walls of stone plugged with TNT. The blinding explosion barricaded the stagecoach and soldiers between a mountain of rubble and the lick and lash of flames.

The tragedy that followed—why, I'll spare you the awful details. 'Tis enough to say the bandit was no amateur, whipping one revolver after another from his saddlebag, draining the cylinders in a strobing, crackling cloud of gun smoke, until only the whinnies of a few horses drifted up from the gully below.

I had in mind to turn about the way we'd come, before that heartless, baby-faced bandit spied us out. But, as sorry luck would have it, Clip-Clop got all spooked by the pistol cracks and broke free of my grasp, galloping into the wilderness below. The clipping and clopping caught the ear of that pyromaniac, who mounted up his steed and galloped towards us, taking aim with a pistol as he charged.

When he halted in front of us, rather than shooting, he let out a high-pitched laugh. He set his pistol in his holster and fit a cigar in the side of his mouth.

At that moment, I knew beyond all doubt who the man must be—none other than the most-wanted scofflaw in the West, Crysco Gringo. He possessed remarkably youthful features—puffy, ruddy cheeks without spot or wrinkle, that piercing laugh unchanged since nursery school, and long eyelashes resembling Venus flytraps. Yea, legend said he could ensnare flies and grasshoppers with the blink of an eye! He appeared so youthful, in fact, that when he began his life of crime in the city of New Orleans, why, the French folks there called him *L'Enfant Terrible*—which means, when translated, The Terrible Child. Later, as he laid waste to banks and pocketbooks throughout the Republic of Texas by way of a clever scheme passing off ordinary rock salt as diamonds, why, he became known as the Crystal Conman, or just plain Crysco for short.

But Crysco was such a slippery criminal that he eluded capture by authorities for the better part of his life, even when they were certain they had him pinned down, hedged in behind and before, with no means of escape. In fact, Crysco was so slippery that, years later, the story went, folks even named a hydrogenated cottonseed oil used in pastries and cupcakes after him. But I digress....

Crysco Gringo, high upon his horse, smiled down at me. "You're worth more alive than dead. I have an important job for you."

The man disgusted me by all I had seen. No amount of bullying and terrorizing would change my mind about that. "We don't want no job from the likes of you, Crysco Gringo."

The baby-faced rider laughed across the bite of his cigar. "So, you know who I am. Well, the only reason I'm sparing your lives today is so you can tell the world who robbed the stagecoach of Santa Anna!"

I said, in disbelief, "You're telling me you just robbed the stagecoach of Antonio Lopez de Santa Anna, the President of Mexico?"

"'Tis as you say!" Crysco bent at the waist, tipping his hat to us. "Santa Anna's three darling daughters—each of them named Maria—plan to wed later this month, in Veracruz, three men named Pedro. Now, the three Pedros aren't brothers—that would be ridiculous—but they are cousins in the same family of wealthy landowners. And so, El Presidente ordered the finest jewelry of Spain and a hundred crates of diamonds shipped in for the occasion. Trouble is, the ship veered off course in a hurricane, took on water in the Gulf of Mexico and ran aground off the coast of New Orleans. I've tracked them along ever since, waiting for the precise moment to strike."

"In that case, I'll take the job! Just so I can see you pay a heavy price for this."

Crysco Gringo, the baby-faced bandit, said nothing, but tugged the reins of his horse, spurring him to gallop toward the stagecoach. Clem and I had little choice but to fetch old Clip-Clop—who was munching flowers trail side a hundred yards ahead—and then set off for the nearest town to tell all who would listen about the murderous exploits of the baby-faced bandit.

We corralled the donkey without struggle about the same time the fire from the blaze died down. Crysco dragged some of the charred logs clear of the trail and commandeered the stagecoach, maneuvering it clear of the debris to inspect its cargo. We were near enough to hear the man carry on about how he had socked it to old Santa Anna as he reached inside the wagon and withdrew a silk purse.

He turned back, shaking it at us. "This is the heavy price I will pay!" And he laughed that nursery school laugh that sent chills through my eyebrows and mustache.

Now, I admit my intrigue got the best of me, drawing my eyes to that purse to see what might be inside. And lo, children, would you believe 'twere a cache of golden earrings encrusted with diamonds and turquoise? Yes, indeed—just as I told you at the start of this story!

Well, Crysco—rather satisfied with the robbery he'd just committed—sealed up the purse and tossed it into the stagecoach. Then, he fastened his own horse to the stagecoach team, uncapped the bota slung about his shoulder and guzzled the water. He wiped his mouth with the back of his hand, then grabbed for his pistols, shooting several shots into the air in celebration, hooting and hollering like he didn't have a care in the world.

'Twould've been better for him if he cared some, for as the pop-pop-pop sounded from his pistols, the horses attached to that stagecoach reared up and galloped full-boar down the trail. Crysco grabbed hold of the rear canvas flap of the coach as they passed but lost his footing in the act. As the stagecoach dragged him along without mercy, skidding and shimmying and rumbling down the rugged trail, the silk purse of earrings became airborne, flying out the back door and into the maelstrom of dust. I spied the purse right away—and so too did Crysco, who tried to snap it out of the air with his Venus flytrap eyelashes. But, having failed at that, Crysco had a decision to make: let go of the flap to retrieve the purse of earrings—risking the loss of the stagecoach filled with a hundred crates of diamonds—or continue to hold on for dear life. Well, 'twas an easy decision for him to make, and so he held on.

As the baby-faced bandit and the runaway stagecoach disappeared down the trail, I grabbed hold of the silk purse filled with the priceless jewelry, knowing there was but one course of action: head south to Veracruz and deliver the earrings to Santa Anna in time for his daughters' weddings.

And so, children, that is precisely what Clementine, Clip-Clop, and I determined to do. 'Twas a long journey, 'twas an arduous journey, but finding favor with the Good Lord Himself, we made our way south to the outskirts of Veracruz the evening before the weddings. From the mountain-top trail, with dusk settling upon the world below, we beheld the splendor of Veracruz lit with torches and bedecked with hanging baskets of wedding flowers. Streamers of white linen billowed from the windows of the Presidential palace.

We rode on toward Veracruz, receiving escort from the General of the Army himself into the courtyard of the Presidential palace. When Santa Anna saw what we had brought, his eyes welled up with a mist of tears, for he loved his three Maria daughters and wanted them to have the finest accouterments on their weddings day. As a reward for our labor of goodness, Santa Anna pledged that when the time came for Clementine's betrothal, why, he'd extend her the same manner of wedding at the Presidential palace he had prepared for his own daughters.

He also offered Clementine any item from the purse of earrings. Now, mark it up to an error by the palace staff back in the Empire of Spain, or divine intervention (I'll let you judge the matter for yourselves, seeing I have my own understanding of these things,) but nestled among those earrings was a single necklace, fashioned from the gears of a clock or similar mechanism. The gears fit together in a peculiar design that reminded me of a thing I could not place my finger on, like déjà vu. Clem chose this exquisite item to fasten around her neck.

Santa Anna accepted the purse of earrings, slipping it into the pocket of his coat. "As for the rest of the cargo, was it not retrieved?"

I removed my hat and placed it over my heart, shaking my head.

"Well, that is regrettable news for the Veracruz orphanage."

His answer perplexed me. "Pray tell, Presidente—what on God's green earth would a house of orphans need with a hundred crates of diamonds?"

"Diamonds?" A maze of wrinkles overwhelmed Santa Anna's face. Then, in sudden understanding, he began to laugh, and laugh, and laugh. Fighting back tears of delight, he said, "Those were not a hundred crates of diamonds. They were a hundred crates of diapers—for the orphans."

And so, dear children, while Crysco Gringo eluded the authorities a while longer—yea, he'd answer in due time for his terrible crimes—we saw that day that the Lord has a sense of humor, rendering temporary justice upon *L'Enfant Terrible* in a most humbling fashion. We also saw that for those of us willing to fight the good fight and persevere to the end, our reward is as sure as the rising of the sun.

Now, getting down to brass tacks, the moral of this story, the very crux of it, is we can do all things through Christ who strengthens us. Or, put another way, as the Good Book does in Isaiah 40:31, *"God strengthens those who trust in Him. They shall mount up with wings like eagles. They shall run wind-sprints and breathe easy. They shall walk and not faint."* And to that you can add, *'They shall stand toe-to-toe with baby-faced bandits and not back down. They shall turn the diamonds of those bandits into diapers!'*

That's how I would've put it had the Lord chosen me to write his word. But then again, I suppose that's why the Lord didn't choose me to write His word. I'd've written something like that that left folks scratching their heads through the ages.

9 BELLATRIX AND THE PHOENIX FEATHER (1849)

"Some said the feather was a good omen of our travels onward to California fields of gold; but the Egyptian, why, he spoke of fortunes far more enticing to the tingling ears of a 49er."

The story I'm fixing to tell you comes from a time when I was on my way to California during the Gold Rush of 1849. My beloved Millicent had passed away two winters before, so it was just me and Clementine the summer of 1849 making our way across the great southwestern desert. Other prospectors were making their way out west, too, all of us seeking our fortunes, and so we traveled together, as seemed good to us, for the sharing of supplies, companionship and mutual protection against the lawless bands of ruffians who roamed the territories in those days.

By early July we had made our way across much of what is now the state of Arizona, and by the evening of July 4th, which is Independence Day, as you know, we reached the Grand Canyon. And what a spectacular sight it was to behold! The wonders of God's handiwork never fail to astonish those who be willing to open their doubting eyes, and this marvel did not disappoint, displaying the power of an ancient deluge to cut through solid rock into the depths of the earth. We pitched our tents overlooking the canyon, watching the sunset turn the clouds all crimson and gold, and I remember the moon shining particularly bright that evening, seeing it was only one day shy of its fullness.

It was in this setting, just after dinnertime, as we sat around the campfire enjoying a freshly steeped pot of dandelion tea, that a rather strong wind kicked up, threatening to snuff out the roaring campfire and blow all our hats into the unfathomable canyon below. But like Sweet Jesus calming the storm on the Sea of Galilee, the wind died off as suddenly as it began! And then, astonishing all who bore witness to these things, an enormous feather about the length of a cubit—which is the distance from the tip of a man's middle finger to the bottom of his elbow—fell out of the starry sky and landed at the feet of a prospector named Phinehas and his daughter Bellatrix.

Now, Phinehas wasn't quite sure what manner of feather it was, be it from an old rugged hawk, a powerful bald eagle, or even a mighty California condor—birds well known to nest in those parts of the canyon. But none of those guesses held much water with old Phinehas, seeing that those birds were black or brown in color, and this feather, when held up to the flames of the campfire, boasted hues of a river, deep and blue, with highlights of ruby-red electrifying the entire vane, from the tip to the afterfeather all the way down to the hollow shaft. And when Phinehas held that feather up high, waving it this way and that in the desert moonlight, hints of fiery gold sparkled in the recesses of those mysterious barbs.

As you might well imagine, plenty of folks there that night held strong opinions on what it was, and these opinions all, more or less, settled on the idea that it came from a wayward parrot or a macaw, blown off course by a hurricane way down in Central America—Costa Rica even. While the theory might've explained the source of the sudden gust of wind, one fellow among us who hailed from the Old World—the country of Egypt, in fact—swore the feather came not from parrot or macaw. Nay, the Egyptian swore it belonged to the most tantalizing bird of ancient lore, the Phoenix!

The way this fellow saw it, the Phoenix had migrated to these parts long ago and built her nest on the craggy side of the canyon walls, where she settled down and promptly burst into flames, as the bird is said to do every 500 years, leaving only that single feather behind, from which one day she would rise again, in all her glory as was before. The wind, he reasoned, dislodged the feather from the ashes in the nest, carrying it, as if by Providence, into the lives of Phinehas and Bellatrix.

For you see, young Avalon, a feather like that would be a mighty valuable feather indeed! Legends abound regarding the mysterious ancient bird called the Phoenix, and you should have heard some of the speculations arising that night about what the feather might mean to the fortunes of Phinehas and his young daughter Bellatrix. Some said the feather was a good omen of our travels onward to fields of California gold; but the Egyptian, why, he spoke of fortunes far more enticing to the tingling ears of a 49er.

He swore, as legend had it, such a feather would grant the one who possessed it powers of invisibility, great length of life and wealth beyond all his wildest imaginations! Furthermore, he claimed whoever held the feather could see something no one else could see—namely, that the Phoenix, just before combusting, had laid herself 500 silver eggs in the nest, one for each year she had soared above the bonds of earth. And the feather, as you might've already guessed, could guide a man all the way back to the nest, like a powerful William Sturgeon electromagnet!

The murmur that erupted from the camp was akin to a vast swarm of bees, everyone chit-chatting, oh-mying, oohing and aahing about invisibility, the fountain of youth and those 500 silver eggs. Why, twasn't long before a great whoop and cry went up from our band of fortune-seekers that we should fire up torches and track down the nest that very minute.

But the old timer Phinehas exercised a steady, reasoned mind where legends were concerned, and after he quieted down the crowd, he reminded us that even with strong moonlight guiding our steps, a nighttime excursion 'cross the desert would be foolhardy and likely to cost some of us dearly—yea, our very lives!

The time to investigate the matter, he said, lay on the other side of night, when we'd enjoy the twin blessings of rest and a shining sun to aid us in our quest. On that advice, he tucked the feather into Bellatrix's hand for safekeeping and shooed the lot of us off to bed.

We all agreed the plan was a good plan—a wise plan—and laid down to dream what fortunes awaited us just beyond the dawn. All of us, that is, save for that yarn-spinning Egyptian. For you see, during the small hours of the night that two-bit rascal crawled the length of the camp on his belly—like the snake he was—to the side of the tent where Bellatrix lay in a deep and satisfying slumber. Then, with his Bowie knife drawn, shimmering in the moonlight, he slit open the tent, reached his long, boney fingers into the confines thereof, and plucked that fabled feather from the cherubic arms of Bellatrix. The instant the treasured possession came into his grasp, he slinked back to the brush line and absquatulated into the night.

Well, at the first light of dawn, when the melancholy chords of birdsong roused Bellatrix from her dreams, and her long-lashed eyes fluttered open, why, she sensed some terrible apocalypse had transpired in the dark of night. And indeed, twasn't long before she realized the feather was gone. She searched this place and that, turning over and inside out all her bedding and her night gown—why, in desperation, she even gave the tresses of her hair a good shake in the off chance the feather had somehow worked its way into tangles thereof. But alas, the feather was truly gone, and it was then she spied the telltale slit in the canvas of the tent, flapping—as if in mockery of her loss—in the dry desert breeze. She let out a shriek that woke the entire camp, causing grown men to burst out of their tents like balls of lead fired from battlefield cannons!

Once we'd gathered our wits and assembled around the fire pit to see what the ruckus was about, we noticed 'twasn't only the feather that had gone missing—no! But also, some of our food rations, one of the pack mules, and the wily silver-tongued Egyptian. Now, some said there was nothing to be done about it, for if the feather imparted the power of invisibility, why, there was no way to see him; therefore, he'd not be heard from again—nay, not until he gave an account of his actions at the great white throne of judgment.

But it occurred to some of us that even a person possessing powers of invisibility, who passed unseen by the eye of man, would leave traces of having come and gone—the same way all of creation, when examined by an unjaundiced eye, reveals the fingerprints of Almighty God who created it. So, as we searched about here and there, we found certain things out of sorts, such as broken twigs in the brush, the lid from a peach-packed mason jar that had gone missing that morning, and footprints, why, about the length and width of the crafty Egyptian.

After examining this forensic evidence before us, we resolved to but one course of action: assemble a posse of strong, able-bodied men, on our most fleet-footed steeds (which is what prospectors call their horses,) and flush that scheming scallywag from his hideout. Yea, even if we had to lift the canyon floor and empty it like a bowl.

Among our ranks—aiding us in this noble task—was none other than a full-blooded, tried-and-true Apache girl, a fearless scout and tracker of the first stripe who, it seemed to us, possessed preternatural powers of perception. Why, it was said she could track the scent of an owl to the dark side of the moon, or one of a catfish buried so deep in mud that its whiskers poked straight out into China—if such things were possible!

Yea, this girl took up the vanguard in our 49er Phalanx—which is what we named our posse, because at the time it sounded like a name that'd strike fear into the heart of a man under hot pursuit. In no time, the fearless Apache girl guided us through fields of rattlesnake infested boulders and over hillsides of fierce scorpions and razor-sharp cacti, until we reached a crevasse at the very rim of the canyon itself.

And there, just beside the crevasse, we encountered the missing pack mule, who looked to be in the fight of his life! His reins stretched taut into the depths of the canyon and his hooves dug relentlessly at the earth but kept giving ground on account of the sandy desert floor. Phinehas leaped off his steed in the nick of time, grabbing hold of those reins and craning his neck over the rim to glimpse what manner of nemesis embattled that brave mule. And do you know what Phinehas saw, dangling from those reins 500 feet up from the canyon floor? That's right! 'Twas the old Egyptian, clinging to the reins for dear life with one hand, while clinging to the feather for shameless greed with the other! Seems he couldn't make up his mind—grab hold of the reins with both hands and pull himself to safety (which would require dropping the feather,) or continue clinging both to the reins and the feather, which would cause him, in short order, to meet his Maker at 9.8 meters per second squared.

Well, Phinehas, being the righteous soul he was, offered the thief a third way, by stretching out his hand and snatching the Egyptian by the wrist, rescuing him from the clutches of the crevasse and the certain death that awaited him! Once the Egyptian was back on solid ground, Phinehas reclaimed the feather from his clutches and without a second thought, let fly with it into the canyon where it was caught up in the draft whence it came, never to be seen again.

And some cried out, 'Oh, Phinehas, how could you throw away the power of invisibility like that?' To which Phinehas replied, 'The only thing invisible here was that man's sin to his own mind.'

And some others cried out, 'But Phinehas, how could you throw away great length of life?' To which Phinehas pointed out, 'What life is longer than the one plucked from a certain grave?'

And still others cried out, 'But great gravy, Phinehas, how could you throw away the dowsing feather to the 500 silver eggs, and wealth beyond all our wildest imaginations?' To which Phinehas raised an eyebrow and smiled, 'What greater wealth hath a man than helping his neighbor in need?'

And it would be an understatement to say, dear children, that our rag-tag band of fortune-seekers—the 49er Phalanx, as we called ourselves—marveled at the wisdom of old Phinehas. But truth be told, 'twasn't his own wisdom at all; he obtained it from a much Higher Source.

Because getting down to brass tacks, the moral of this story, the very crux of it, is that sin is a great weight about the neck of every human being, threatening to pull us all into the unforgiving pit, and no talisman or ritual in this world can save us from that—nay, only the blood of Jesus. For as it is written, *"Give wickedness the boot and follow after God."* And that bit of wisdom, as you might know, and I'm certain you do since you're all sharp as whips, comes straight from the Good Book itself, 2 Kings 17:13-14 to be precise.

10 EXODUS FROM ANGEL'S CAMP (1849)

"We were trapped there with no means of escape—not so much as a strap of leather beneath the soles of our feet—forced into a condition no different from slavery."

In October of 1849, having made our way through the Grand Canyon and up out of the New Mexico territory (as settlers called it in those days,) Clem and I reached the gold fields of California, settling down in a place called Angel's Mining Camp.

The camp was named for the brothers Henry and George Angel, who served as soldiers in the Mexican-American War, but upon the resolution of that conflict, they determined to try their hands at gold prospecting, buying up a promising tract of land in Calaveras County. As it happened, the Angel brothers liked the idea of gold prospecting more than the back-breaking labor of prospecting itself. So, they sold the property to a close relation of theirs, a man by the name of Ichabod Othenio, who was not an angel in either name or disposition. For you see, dear children, under Ichabod Othenio's management, the once promising mining camp succumbed to deplorable conditions of his own making, resembling a prison camp at its end.

But Clem and I and the other miners knew nothing of these things when we arrived there seeking our fortunes. No! We were lured by the promise of easy gold, secure lodging, three squares a day, fair weekly wages and the unequivocal guarantee we'd share in the profits of the mine. The only stipulation was we must sign three-year contracts to labor there and nowhere else, to ensure a steady workforce to get that gold out of the ground.

Only once we signed our names to the paper, why, the foremen employed by Ichabod—taskmasters, as we called them—seized our shoes and held our tools as communal property. Then, to drive salt in the open wound, they hacked our wages in half. What stiver remained was taken by Ichabod to pay for our food and lodging!

We endured these harsh conditions for the better part of a year, hoping against hope that our lot would improve with each new extraction of ore from the mine. But Ichabod segregated the operations in such a way that no one really knew how much gold was coming out of the mine. We suspected, however, more came out than we received back in profit sharing. All of which is to say, we were trapped there with no means of escape—not so much as a strap of leather beneath the soles of our feet—forced into a condition no different from slavery.

As any blind Bartamaeus could see coming, a grumbling arose from the miners that they could endure the conditions no longer. They sought to petition Ichabod for a day of rest, as the Good Book calls for, when we could take our minds off the depths of the earth and fix them squarely on Heaven above. They spoke of venturing outside the camp to a place—about three hours to the east—where a lazy little river snaked its way through the valley.

Now, we deliberated over these things around the evening campfire for a fortnight, making little headway on a course of action. We feared what Ichabod's response might be to the request. Many men feared the loss of not only their livelihoods—but yea, their very lives! That is until Clementine, my darling daughter, tender little thing that she was, stood up tall and true, like a mighty redwood among reeds blowing in the wind. She said, "Since God has commanded us to take a Sabbath rest, shouldn't we trust in Him to make a way for us, to do as He asks?"

This simple logic, children, had the effect of cutting straight to the hearts of the most wobbly-kneed miners among us, so that in nothing flat we resolved to petition Ichabod in the morning. But then the question arose as to who'd serve as the mouthpiece for our group before our taskmaster. Well, a few of the more well-read gentlemen pointed out that in the Bible, when decisions needed to be made, men cast lots—which I suppose is like rolling dice or drawing straws. So, that's precisely what we did.

Dear children, I don't know what it is about me and the casting of lots, but every time I'm involved in the process, the lot seems to fall squarely on my head! And 'twas no different this time than any other.

Now, I'm not the most persuasive of speakers, nor am I much to look at, but the other miners figured I'd do until such a fellow arrived. They spurred me on my way to petition Ichabod for a weekly respite, a Sabbath day, if you will, and bade me Godspeed to that end.

I brought Clementine along with me, too, for I don't mind saying that I felt a mite weak in the knees myself, and I longed to harbor inside of me the childlike faith she exhibited. As we entered Ichabod's office, I removed my hat, placed it over my heart and said a quick prayer to the Lord that whatever came of this meeting, His will be done.

"Mr. Othenio, us miners been discussing the fact that we ain't had a Sabbath day's rest since we entered camp. Now, seeing as the Lord hath commanded us to take our rest, we felt it good to petition you for a respite that we might journey three hours to the east, to a sleepy little river where we might—well, you know—worship God."

Ichabod said, "A sleepy little river? Why, that's all lazy talk! If you have so much time on your hands that you can go hiking across every mountain and valley this side of the Mississippi, then perhaps your work ain't hard enough for you, now is it?"

Ichabod commanded his taskmasters that we should deliver our daily quota of ore out without the benefit of rail barrows, which were the carts we used to move the ore out of the mine.

So, the next day we slaved away, from sunup to sundown, carrying rocks in the gathering of our shirts and the depths of all our pockets, but 'tweren't no use—the taskmasters badgered us as to why we couldn't make our daily quota of ore.

What's worse, some of the miners turned against me, blaming me for speaking to Ichabod in the first place, pining away that they didn't mind being slaves after all. Well, this stuck in my craw. I couldn't let it go! I went back to Ichabod, petitioning him once again to let us journey to the sleepy little river three hours to the east.

But Ichabod weren't having none of it, insisting we were the laziest bunch of miners in all of California—yea, maybe the entire world (as if he could know such a thing.) Instead of letting us go, he ordered his taskmasters to take away our shovels and pick axes but continue to deliver our daily quota of ore by digging it out of the mine with our bare hands.

Oh, you should have heard the wailing and gnashing of teeth the next day! Just about all the miners blamed me for the ill that had befallen us. Perhaps another man would have given into their cries and begged Ichabod to keep us as slaves the rest of our natural lives. But here's something you ought to know about me if you don't already know it, children—I can be a stubborn old coot. Considering Clementine's innocent eyes, I knew I couldn't back down from this. It was just the way it had to be.

So, I presented myself to Ichabod the next day, like I was Holy Moses himself. "Let my miners go, that we may worship the Lord by the sleepy river, or I fear His wrath may be a-kindled against you."

And lo-and-behold, 'twas at the very moment that one of Ichabod's foremen bounded into the office, his face white as a ghost, saying: "The sluice has turned to blood!" (Now, if you don't know what a sluice is, why, it's sort of like a man-made river where we tumbled the ore to shake out nuggets of gold.)

When Ichabod heard the cries of his foreman, he scoffed, theorizing that the ore must be iron rich and a tad on the rusty side, which explained the illusion. Anyhow, it didn't change his mind none about us leaving camp. That was the first day of the Lord working on Ichabod's heart.

And on we slaved.

The second day I returned the same as before, saying: "Let my miners go, that we may worship the Lord by the sleepy river, or I fear His wrath may be a-kindled against you, as when He turned the sluice to blood."

And lo-and-behold, a foreman bounded into the office, his eyes as big as Liberty dollars, shouting: "The sluice is filled with frogs! Frogs are leaping in and out like it's the end of the world!"

Ichabod scoffed at this too, saying it had been a tad on the dry side as of late and the frogs were just migrating to the nearest water source. Anyhow, it didn't change his mind none about us leaving camp.

And on we slaved.

The third day I returned the same as before, saying: "Let my miners go, that we may worship the Lord by the sleepy river, or I fear His wrath may be a-kindled against you, as when He caused frogs to multiply in the sluice."

And lo-and-behold, the foreman bounded in, leaping and scratching every inch of his body, saying: "All the foremen have lice, the dang buggers are chewing us alive!"

Ichabod scoffed at this too, saying: "Tell them to wash off in the sluice." But the foreman said they couldn't on account of the frogs. And yea, I did see Ichabod scratch behind his ear and then rake his fingernails through his bushy beard. Even so, it didn't change his mind none about us leaving camp.

And on we slaved.

The fourth day I returned as before, reiterating my fear about the Lord's wrath and mentioning the sleepy river once again.

And then we heard a great buzzing outside the office and heard a whoop and holler from the foremen by the mines. We looked out the window to see a black swarm of flies chasing them around. Now, I'd like to say this changed old Ichabod's steely heart, but 'tweren't no different than before.

And on we slaved.

The fifth day I returned the same as before, urging Ichabod to let the miners go, lest the Lord Almighty kindle His wrath against him.

The foremen slouched into the office, his head bowed and his hat upon his chest, saying: "The animals—the donkeys, the horses, the chickens—they're all sick!"

And not only sick, dear children, but many of them died that day, so many, in fact, that we had to forsake our quota and leave the mines to bury the dead animals.

And on we slaved.

And on went this pattern, so that on the sixth day, boils broke out over the foreman and Ichabod, too.

On the seventh day, thunder and hail struck Angel's Camp.

On the eighth day, locusts descended out of the blue sky and ravaged the vegetation in the camp, scaring the living daylights out of the foremen!

And on the ninth day, round the time the lunch bell tolled, darkness fell upon the camp, so that the foremen stumbled around, bumping into one another and stubbing their toes on chairs and tables. They were as blind as men without lanterns on a moonless night!

Finally, on the tenth day, the foremen arose to find the first-hatched of all the chickens in the camp, rolled over on their backs with their talons sticking straight in the air, dead.

Ichabod, drawn from his slumber by the wails of the foremen, beheld his favorite pet chicken, one that slept faithfully at his feet for years, deader than his dusty old boots! So with that, dear children, Ichabod implored us to leave camp and journey those three hours over mountains and valleys, to the sleepy river where we might rest our weary bones and worship God. He returned our shoes to us that we might make haste. His foremen returned our tools, too, and filled our pockets with gold nuggets, entreating us to go and worship the Lord and never come back. Not needing to hear it twice, we did just that, at last escaping the treachery of Ichabod Othenio, hoping to find a new hope beyond Angel's Camp where we might at long last make our fortunes.

So, getting down to brass tacks, the moral of this story, the very crux of it, is that faith gives you courage to do what you should even when you don't feel ready. Or, as we like to say in the mining camp, *"Be strong and brave. Do not be afraid of the kick of a mule, even if it costs you your teeth. Do not lose hope. For the Lord your God is with you wherever you go."*

11 RIDDLES OF THE CANYON SPHINX (1849)

"This was an extraordinary statue, for as soon as we set our sights upon it, the Sphinx turned its head, casting upon us the gaze of those stone-dead eyes as if we were prey."

As I shared with you in times past, dear children, in the fall of 1849, me and Clementine and a host of miners were held against our wills in Angel's Mining Camp by a merciless taskmaster named Ichabod Othenio. But after a series of plagues struck the camp, Ichabod saw fit to release his laborers from their drudgery to travel three days eastward to a sleepy little river in a valley where we might worship God and observe the Sabbath rest.

But not long after we fled Angel's Camp, Ichabod Othenio, cruel taskmaster that he was, had a change of heart and decided he'd made a colossal error by letting his laborers go free. So, he rounded up a band of unscrupulous ruffians—or, better said, he hired a group of men who didn't care one wit about the law, but always chose wrong over right—to track down our caravan and return us to Angel's Camp, shackled in cold steel chains!

As fate had it, though, a merchant galloping past the ruffians overheard their plans against us. Upon reaching our redoubt, he urged us to make haste to the east, away from the ruffians. We packed up from the sleepy little river to avoid any conflict, only to be met by several 49ers heading in the opposite direction, that is, back toward the ruffians. They implored us not to go the way they'd come, describing an all-out war raging in the east between Americans and Indians, with folks shooting first and asking question later.

You see, the encroachment of fortune-seekers in the West had become too much for the Indians to bear. Suspicions existed on every side. Too many folks considered all interactions with the Indians improper. Yea, in some circles, 'twas considered an abomination to so much as smile at an Indian.

Out there in the desert, our supplies running dangerously low, beset on both sides by ruffians and Indian warriors, we settled down for the night to consider our next move. We gathered twigs and sagebrush for a campfire, then set to eating prickly pear cactus and whatever bugs we could dig out of the earth. Yes, indeed—those were lean, desperate times!

I'd like to say spirits were high in our caravan on account of escaping the clutches of that no-good taskmaster of

Angel's Camp, Ichabod Othenio, but 'twasn't the case. With blistered feet, sun-scorched skin and rumbling stomachs from a lack of good eats, spirits sank about as low as the grave. Yea, the most common phrase uttered in the camp was, "Woe is me!"

Under these stark conditions, someone had the noble idea we should trade adventure stories around the campfire— that is, stories of better times that would uplift our spirits from the doldrums. And so, one man after another shared a story from the Gold Rush, tales intended to take our minds off our present dire circumstances before facing grim reality once again. When the turn fell to me, why, without thinking, I spewed on and on about mine and Clementine's first pass through the Grand Canyon on our way to the California fields of gold.

I told them of Phinehas and his daughter Bellatrix and the finding of that Phoenix feather. I told them of the wily Egyptian who stole the feather in hopes of dowsing with it to find the Phoenix's nest, said to conceal 500 silver eggs. I told them of the 49er Phalanx and how we chased down the thief just in the nick of time to save him from plummeting to his death. And I told of how Phinehas threw that Phoenix feather into the wind because of the greed he saw it brought upon our caravan.

And I must say, children, the mood in the camp did change, from one of despair to one of vim and vigor. So much so that before long, someone asked what we were doing wandering in the desert, beset by ruffians and Indian warriors, sobbing ourselves silly when we could be sniffing out those 500 silver eggs in the Grand Canyon?

Yes, indeed—all present seemed to agree it was the best prospect going for us. I protested, telling the men how ugly things turned in times past over those 500 silver eggs, but no one cared to hear me spin my adventure story of unfound riches into a cautionary tale. No! Now, Clem and I could've gone our separate way from the caravan, but the desert is a hard place on your own, especially when danger lurks behind every cactus and sun-bleached carcass. I had Clementine's well-being to think about, too, so we continued with the group, into the mysteries of the Grand Canyon.

'Tis important for you'ns to understand that the Indians in the canyon kept a watchful eye on all travelers coming and going, and a group our size did catch their attention. The chief of these Indians, a man by the name of White Feather, who, unbeknownst to us had converted to Christianity some years before—yea, he and all his tribe—sent forth scouts to discover our intentions. He suspected we were either soldiers come to do battle, or miners looking to lay dynamite in the canyon, but what the scouts saw was a bunch of men scaling cliffs, rifling through every bird's nest they happened upon. Truth be told, they didn't know what to make of our odd behavior.

But that's not all they reported back to White Feather. For you see, one morning, just before breakfast, the scouts had witnessed me and Clem kneeling to say prayers and studying the Scriptures. Well, this encouraged White Feather to see others of the faith in the canyon, enough, in fact, to send forth his two scouts yet again, this time to welcome us back to their camp.

You see, while White Feather and his tribe had converted to the faith some years before, they were without the Scriptures, and they all longed to learn more than what they had first received. They were hoping I could read some of it to them.

The next day, while the other fortune-seekers risked their necks scaling the canyon walls, uprooting bird's nests and getting dive-bombed by angry condors, Clem and I set out along the Colorado River in search of a promising place to pan for gold. As we walked, there in the distance, we spied a horseshoe shaped bend in the river that wrapped around a crag. Indeed, it looked about as promising a stretch of river as any stretch we'd ever laid eyes upon. We quickened our pace, anticipating finding gold deposits beyond all our wildest imaginations.

But as we neared the bend in the river, out from a cave hidden in the canyon wall sprang two Indian warriors, looking about as surly and fierce as any two you ever had the misfortune to face! Startled, Clem and I halted, not sure whether to run or to charge, but our fear got the best of us, and so we stood where we stood on the banks of the river, shaking at the knees. One of the Indians held up his hand. Then, to our astonishment, he spoke in our own tongue.

"Chief White Feather wishes to meet with you. He desires to learn whatever wisdom God has laid upon your heart. Come at once!"

Now, you children are young, but I'm sure you are observant enough to see that people who are different from each other tend to stay apart. It's a sad fact that plagues us since the fall of the Tower of Babel, so I wasn't keen on traveling with these scouts back to their camp. I figured 'twas best if we just stuck with our own kind. I'm ashamed to say such things were in my heart, but I'm telling you how it was.

I told the scouts, "'Tain't customary for Americans and Indians to have anything to do with each other. Given the recent tensions between our peoples, I'd just as soon keep it that way." I motioned to Clem, and we pushed past the Indian scouts, walking around the horseshoe bend.

And here's where the story gets mighty interesting, children, for as we rounded that bend, lo, we laid eyes upon a sight we never expected to see this side of the Atlantic Ocean. Nay! We rubbed our eyes bloodshot to be sure we were seeing what we saw. For there, high up on the crag, chiseled out of stone, loomed a statue of that terrifying creature of old, the terrible songstress known as the Sphinx!

I do not exaggerate when I tell you she spanned fifty feet from her haunches to her nose. Now, this Sphinx was a tad different from the one on the Giza plateau in Egypt you might've learned about from your schoolmarms (if indeed they teach such things anymore,) seeing that it had the body of a lion, the head of a human, the horns of an ox and the wings of an eagle—a right fearsome-looking creature no matter that it was made of stone.

To be sure, this was an extraordinary statue, for as soon as we set our sights upon it, the Sphinx turned its head, casting upon us the gaze of those stone-dead eyes as if we were prey. And it said,

"All who wish to pass beneath,
Must solve my riddles or feed my teeth."

Well, I don't mind telling you that this old-timer has faced life and death battles in his days, from escaping the death roll of a twenty-foot gator to wrestling a great white shark for ten—nay, 15—minutes beneath the waves until he cried uncle! But when I heard this stone beast say what she said, why, I felt about as naked and alone as a baby sparrow that ain't yet learned to fly when a raccoon shows up unannounced for dinner. Yes, indeed! I looked back for the Indian warriors, only to find them hiding behind a boulder.

They beckoned to us, saying, "Don't take her challenge—no one has ever answered her riddles correctly. She'll chew you up!"

What I did next might sound strange to you, children, as surely as it sounds strange to my own ears saying it, but my mind was fixed on that rotten idea that 'twas a sin to associate with those Indians. Now, I want you to think about this sin entangling me for a moment, for it told me 'twas better to face that dreaded Sphinx, whom none had defeated by solving her riddles, than it was to accept the scout's invitation to preach the Gospel in Indian country. As I said before, I'm ashamed to admit that's the way it was, but I'm telling you the way it was, so you might learn from my mistakes. As such, facing down the Sphinx seemed my only option.

Then again, it might have been pure and simple greed that clouded my judgment, for it crossed my mind that whoever constructed this remarkable statue must've done so to guard a treasure of unimaginable worth.

I said to her, "Tell me your riddles."

Even though that statue's eyes were carved from solid stone, I affirm to you they glowed the color of flame when I took the challenge. And I also affirm to you I interpreted that color as the color of hunger.

The beast said,

> *"There is a creature in this world*
> *Whose feet are four and two and three,*
> *When he goes upon all four*
> *The slowest pace doth goeth he.*
> *What is the creature?"*

Now, this riddle perplexed me, seemed crazy even, but the longer I thought about it the surer I was that I knew the answer.

"The creature is a man," I said, "who crawls on all fours as a baby, moves on two legs as an adult, and walks with a cane in old age. As a baby, going on all fours, he is the slowest."

The Sphinx was silent for an extended span of time, so long, in fact, that I questioned my own sanity, questioned whether I had imagined this statue having ever spoken to me. Until she said,

"Though you seem to have some skill,
It only whets my urge to kill."

At this point, one would think I'd raise my hand and ask to be excused from the rest of the challenge, just turn tail and return to my business of panning for gold in some other nook of the canyon. But after correctly answering that first riddle, why, I was puffed up with pride, feeling invincible, as it were, so I said, "Enough threats. Tell me your next riddle."

It said to me,

"There are two sisters in this world
The first one is her sister's mom,
The second sister, not outdone
Gave birth at dawn to her own mom.
Who are the sisters?"

I pondered this riddle more deeply than the first, as it seemed to be all nonsense—a riddle with no answer, just a ploy to twist words into such knots that I would submit to her, that we would become her next meal. But as I turned the riddle over in my head, I looked to Clementine, who was doing the same. And then Clem's eyes grew wide, and she mouthed a single word—*dawn*—and like the coming of dawn, the answer flooded her mind and her eyes like light.

Clementine blurted, "The sisters are day and night!"

The Sphinx quavered at this answer, and small cracks appeared in the stone around her eyes and upon her brow. Yea, we heard the snapping of its face echo on the canyon walls.

She said,

> *"None have ever come this far,*
> *With riddle three I raise the bar."*

Sensing that riches beyond my wildest imaginations were within snatching distance, I said, "Enough games, Sphinx. Ask us your riddle!"

And that is when she said,

> *"There are two brothers in this world*
> *Between them lies an ocean wide,*
> *So rough the waves and fierce the winds*
> *That all who tried to cross have died.*
> *None have ever crossed that water*
> *And yet both men have the same father.*
> *How can this be?"*

As the last syllable fell from her tongue, I staggered, dropping to one knee. Dear children, I was overcome with grief, for I knew the answer, and I wept bitterly.

She cried out, *"Answer me!"*

I pawed at the tears in my eyes as Clementine helped me to my feet. I recalled how my father had died in the Great Plains Fire of 1824, unable to reconcile with his neighbor, and I said, "The answer is plain—the ocean is pride, and the two brothers are me and Chief White Feather. God is our Father!"

With that answer, the Sphinx let out a terrible roar that quaked the canyon, ushering an avalanche of rocks down the crag and into the river below. The fearsome songstress, whose only movement prior to this had been to pivot her head and burnish her lips, recoiled on her haunches and vaulted from the perch, dashing her body onto the boulders below, shattering into a thousand lackluster stones.

And with the Sphinx destroyed, I had a decision to make. I had earned the right to safe passage around the horseshoe bend, to discover what treasures that fearsome creature guarded, but my heart was a calling me in the opposite direction, toward the Indian scouts. Now, does anyone care to guess what I chose to do? That's right, I followed the scouts to their camp, because at last I understood that God is no respecter of persons, which is to say, God doesn't play favorites with anyone because of what he looks like or where he comes from.

That decision to follow the call of God, dear children, made all the difference in the world, for it opened a door to a lifelong friendship with White Feather and his tribe, folks I never would've given the time of day were it not for that encounter with the Canyon Sphinx at the horseshoe bend. And as for the treasure guarded by the Canyon Sphinx, of which I am sure you are eager to learn what became of it, why, I suppose I must save that tale for another day.

For getting down to brass tacks, the moral of this story, the very crux of it, is that when the task before you seems impossible, push ahead with all your might. Or, as we like to say in the mining camp, *"Don't get tired of shaking that pan. At the right time, you will strike it rich if you don't give up."*

12 A MIGHTY PAIR OF BOOTS (1851)

"The current swept me along the ladder of the sluice, smashing me this way and that against the banks like a dead fish. I blinked in and out of consciousness until at last it seemed the world did end."

I t is said that beauty is in the eye of the beholder, that one man's trash is another man's treasure, that the best things in life aren't things at all... but it is also said the journey of a thousand miles begins with a single step, and I'm here to tell you that if you plan to take a journey of a thousand miles anytime soon, you best lace onto your feet a mighty pair of boots with unbreakable leather laces!

Now, the tale from my journal I wish to share with you today comes from the spring of 1851, shortly after Clementine and I arrived at that mining town in the Sierra Nevada mountains where sluicing was the primary method used to recover gold from the mines. I was spending a good fourteen, sixteen... nay, twenty-eight hours a day slaving over the sluice to recover a single flake of gold no bigger than my least favorite pinky nail—which would be my left one!

Working alongside me was a man by the name of old Jacob Waltz, whom I've mentioned a time or two in the past, but when the events of this story occurred, why, he was all but unknown to me, just another prospector in search of his fortune.

I don't mind telling you that I didn't much care for old Jacob Waltz when I first met him, namely because he went about sluicing with a scowl on his face—never satisfied—and when we'd sit down to eat, he'd complain that the bread was too hard, or the soup was too salty, or there was too much sand and too many snails in his mug of water. Oh, how that man complained!

And like me, he had a young child he was attempting to rear own, a fragile little waif of a boy he called Bubby, but whose Christian name was Jacob Waltz, Jr., and this boy always seemed to be on the opposite side of good graces with his old man.

Jacob Waltz spent his days yelling at the young boy, telling him to straighten up, to put his back (what little of it there was) into his labors, to pull his weight or face a dinnerless trip to bed, or worse, a tanning of the hide he wouldn't soon forget. And all this yelling and strife and commotion around the sluice had the effect of wearing me down, of agitating me, until I was just about at the breaking point.

Now, dear children, far be it from me to tell another man how to rear his progeny, but I was at wits end with the man over his maltreatment of the boy, and I did not enjoy the luxury of addressing the matter with Mrs. Jacob Waltz, the mother of the poor lad. Like my darling Clementine, the little waif Bubby no longer had a mother in the world, seeing as she'd passed on to her reward during childbirth.

That said, the day came when we were six or eight or thirty-five hours into our sluicing duties that storm clouds were a rolling in and old Jacob Waltz began badgering Bubby to pick up his pace, to keep his eyes this way but not that, to tuck in his shirt, to roll up his sleeves, to show a little respect for the Waltz family name, to work like he meant it, to do a thousand things 'tweren't possible for a young boy to do even if you threatened to turn loose a pack of wild dogs upon him.

I blurted out, "Great gravy, Jacob Waltz. Cut the young'un some slack. A storm's fixing to roll through and we best stand clear of the sluice at a time like this."

For you see, when a storm like that blew up, why, the sluice was liable to overflow with a surge of water or burst apart at the joints and wash away the hillside. But as it happened, old Jacob Waltz was churning the water with a paddle, trying to speed up the process, when his paddle turned up a great glittering of gold! Why, by the initial look of things, he'd turned up more gold than we'd seen in the past month or more.

As the rain fell, first as a pitter-patter, then as a great cloudburst accompanied by flashes of lightning and great thunderclaps, Jacob barked for Bubby to get this and get that, to go here but not there, to keep his eyes on the prize while not looking to the left or to the right, all the while entreating young Bubby to look alive!

Needless to say, the boy got all flustered and confused, and in his confusion, he climbed into the sluice with a bucket and cheesecloth, trying to strain out the flakes to make his old man proud.

Unfortunately for Bubby, the downpour loaded up the sluice with an avalanche of rain, bearing down like a freight train on him before he even had time to think—yea, before he had time to say, "Oh no, maybe climbing inside of the sluice in a downpour rivaling Noah's wasn't such a good idea!"

And lo-and-behold, the raging waters lifted Bubby off his feet and swept him along with the current down the mountainside.

Now, children, you should know at this point of the story I wasn't always the hunched-over, gray, enfeebled miner you see me as today. No! In those days, I was in the prime of my life, a marvelous specimen of a man more muscular and athletic than any long-haired Samson, fleet-footed Leonidas or hatchet-wielding Paul Bunyan... combined!

I dove into the waters, swimming with such speed that a sonic boom rattled the canyon, and I reached Bubby in the nick of time, grabbing hold of him and tossing him clear of the sluice to safety.

Now, in spite of my preternatural strength, the current swept me along the ladder of the sluice, smashing me this way and that against the banks like a dead fish. Blinking in and out of consciousness, at last it seemed the world did end. Yea—I felt myself become lighter than air as my body seemed to float out of the rapids onto to dry ground.

In reality, however, a couple of miners downstream had seen me floating face-first in the water and fished me out with a lasso about the ankle. As banged up and beaten as I was, twasn't the worst part of my ordeal. No! For it seems the raging current had stripped me of every last stitch of clothing until I was as naked as the day I was born. Not even my boots remained!

Now, my rescuers shielded their eyes from me as they wrapped me in an old burlap potato sack, which seemed like a robe fit for a king in that moment of embarrassment. And thus, in this condition, mangled and cold, barefooted and bedraggled, I hobbled up the mountain path, back to the camp where I sat down in my potato sack before the village fire pit, to dry my soggy bones.

Perhaps this sort of misfortune has happened to you before, and so you can sympathize with me, but for those of you who cannot, imagine, if you will, the prospect of wearing an itchy burlap sack for a week until traders from the town of San Francisco arrived with new clothes and boots. I dreaded the thought but resolved to be grateful for what I had.

Much to my surprise, however, Jacob Waltz appeared at the fire pit, saying I could borrow his boots, seeing that he had an extra pair back at his lodgings. What a welcome treasure those boots were, of more value than a pound of gold! But, what old Jacob Waltz really meant to say, I would learn in time, was that I could borrow his boots even though they were the only pair he owned.

Now, you might wonder why a man would lend the only pair of boots he owned to a man he hardly knew, especially seeing that the paths along the sluice were jagged and beset by brier and tares and leaping, venomous scorpions. When I asked old Jacob Waltz about this later, he confided he'd endured so much pain in this world that he was wont to ease the pain of others, even if it meant absorbing a pressed down, running over, heaping measure of that pain himself.

As I fastened the boots to my feet—with the leather laces crisscrossing one another up the bridge and yet retaining enough slack after threading the last eyelet to wrap around the back of my ankles, twice, and still tie a double knot in front— it occurred to me that a good pair of boots was much like a faithful friend. Such a friend sticks close, lending support through every step of your journey no matter how hard the going gets. Ruminating on these things, I recalled a Bible verse I memorized way back in Sunday school. 'Twas the wisdom of Solomon set down in the Book of Ecclesiastes, when he wrote: "Two are better than one, because they have a good reward for their labor. For if they fall, the one will lift up his fellow: but woe to him that is alone when he falleth; for he hath not another to help him up! And if one prevails against him, two shall withstand him; and a threefold cord is not quickly broken."

To wit, a wise man once said if you truly want to understand another man, try walking in his boots for a mile— whatever no-good thoughts you might have about him are likely to melt away like the frost on a sunny spring day, and you might just change your opinion of him!

Now, children, since we've been talking about things that've been written and said, I don't mind telling you that it has also been said that hindsight is always twenty-twenty (and if you don't know what that means, ask your parents to explain it to you), and I suppose that, looking back, I now understand the mighty pair of boots with unbreakable leather laces was less a thing to cherish than was old Jacob Waltz's expression of love for our Great God and Savior in Heaven above!

For you see, only by striving to emulate (that means to be like) Jesus Himself was old Jacob Waltz able to honor me the way he did. Just imagine the terrible condition my feet would've suffered had Jacob Waltz not come to my rescue that day long ago!

So, getting down to brass tacks, the moral of this story, the very crux of it, is that you ought to honor others by putting their needs ahead of your own. Or, as the Good Book tells it, in Romans 12:10, *"Pour out your love one to another as those who shared their mother's womb, in honor preferring the other as first born!"*

Now pray tell, dear children, do you think old Jacob Waltz could have used that mighty pair of boots along the jagged paths of the sluice, beset by brier and tares and leaping, venomous scorpions? Indeed! And do you think he honored me by allowing my decrepit, sweaty feet to inhabit his trusty boots for a week? Why, yes—yes indeed! And do you think he honored me more than himself by suffering for a spell so that I could enjoy a small measure of comfort in such a distressing, and humbling, time? Well, of course he did!

And that kind of kindness extended to me in my hour of need, dare I say, was of far greater value than a pound—yea, of many pounds of gold!

13 THE GARDEN OF CLEMENTINE (1851)

"That summer of 1851, the grasshoppers came in a swarm the likes of which we hadn't seen in those parts before—nay, nor did we ever after. They settled down on our camp, chewing up the crops, and the blankets we'd thrown over the crops, and the harnesses off the horses, and the paint off our shovels and wagons—why, they even ate the wool off one fellow's sheep!"

D ear children, I've joined you on many occasions to share with you some of the more fascinating tales and trials that swirled about my treasure-seeking, from lost mines to magical bird feathers to ancient civilizations submerged beneath the turbulent indigo seas!

And you might have noticed that I always seemed to find what I went after, but I'm here to tell you 'twasn't always like that. No! There were times of drought and famine and scarcity of gold that could truly humble a man—yea, if only he had eyes to see.

And such was the summer of 1851 when Clementine and I settled down for a spell in a mining town of the Sierra Nevada mountains.

At that time, we were searching for the tiniest bits of gold we could find, wherever we could hope to find 'em. The gold we all read about in the newspapers—fist-sized nuggets that 49ers found just laying out on the ground for the taking—were all long gone, so we had to come up with a different strategy in order to make our fortunes.

Yes, indeed, children, 'twas said in those days a man could find more gold sweeping and dust-panning the floorboards of a jewelry store in Hoboken, New Jersey than he could ever hope to find panning the mountain rivers of California; which wasn't quite true, but 'tis close enough to make the point I'm aiming to make today.

The strategy to which we resorted was to build ourselves a sluice alongside a river, which we did by digging out a hillside like a set of stairs, framing it with wood planks, then diverting part of the river down those stairs. Next, we'd crush up stones we'd blasted out of the mines—back-breaking work, wielding sledgehammers and shovels from sunup to sundown—then mix the rubble with quicksilver before dumping it down the sluice. Now, if you never heard of quicksilver, you might know it by its other name—mercury.

Yea, 'tis a liquid metal you've probably seen in your grandmammy's thermometer.

Now, if you don't know the first thing about what happens when you go mixing quicksilver with gold, well, let me educate you: the mercury sticks to the gold, making it the heaviest thing in the river, causing it to sink, and once you dam up the sluice and let it run dry, why, that mercury and gold amalgam is all that's left behind. Once you gather up that amalgam, you throw it into the flames of a right big fire where the heat burns off the mercury, leaving only precious gold behind. This sluicing business may sound all well and good to folks who ain't got so much as a turnip between the ears, but I'm here to tell you 'tis a horrible thing. You'll learn to regret it!

For you see, when you start dumping mercury into those rivers and streams, why, it acts just like a poison to the fish swimming in there. Soon enough, those fish you relied upon for breakfast, lunch and dinner ain't swimming there no more - no! They're floating down the sluice as dead as the deadest fish you ever seen... or smelled! Such is the situation in which we found ourselves after forging ahead with our sluicing scheme.

Compounding our misfortune, we struggled with our crops that year. You see, in the mining camps back then we relied no small bit on vegetable gardens to supplement what food we speared, hooked and netted from the rivers, or received time to time from the San Francisco merchants working the mining trails.

Now, in our vegetable gardens we used a planting method the Indians called Three Sisters, where you plant some corn, then as soon as it stands a foot high you plant beans next to it, so that when the beans sprout they climb the corn stalks, and finally you plant squash around the corn and beans so that their big leaves fan across the ground and choke any weeds fixing to root in the soil. Cleverest thing you ever saw! But the problem that year had to do with a new group of settlers to the area, a vicious hoard known as the grasshoppers.

That summer of 1851 they came in a swarm the likes of which we hadn't seen in those parts before—nay, nor did we ever after. They settled down on our camp one evening, chewing the crops, and the blankets we'd thrown over the crops, and the harnesses off the horses, and the paint off our shovels and wagons—why, they even ate the wool off one fellow's sheep!

This predicament caused not a few of us in camp to cry out, "Woe is us!" and pine away for a time when we might shovel manure out of a barn in exchange for room and board. But, dear children, such a life has no risk or glory to it, which is what, in addition to gold, we were all searching for in that California mining camp in 1851.

The combination of a paucity of both food and gold—which is another way of saying we didn't have much of either—led us to take stock of what we did have and reflect on what it was we truly wanted out of this life.

For me, I decided that I could get busy living, or get busy dying. So, I reached into my boots and pulled out some old potato skins I'd tucked round about by the heels so I'd have a good fit and wouldn't get blisters. And sure enough, some of those old potato skins had eyes on them!

Now I don't mean they had eyes on them like you and me have eyes on us so we can look at each other. No! But potato eyes are just a funny name we have for those little bumps that are growing points for future potatoes.

And so, I buried those potato skins deep in the garden scoured to the roots by those blasted grasshoppers and prayed for a good crop to come forth in the Lord's time. I also prayed that any potatoes that grew wouldn't smell or taste like my feet! Because let me tell you, children, I can guarantee you'd rather go hungry than smell my feet.

As I did my gardening and said my prayers for sweet smelling potatoes, Clementine stood by quietly—holding a pail of water in her hands—just watching me go about my business. Behind her lingered a lanky boy about her same age, a boy by the name of Jacob Waltz, Jr., whom everybody called "Bubby." 'Twas no secret, Bubby had something of a thing for her.

Now, when I say he had a thing for her, I think all you boys out there know what I mean. If you don't, well, you soon enough will—that is to say, you'll behold a young girl and think she's about the prettiest creature you ever gazed upon; in fact, that's the way I was with my lovely bride Millicent. Before long, you'll get all tongue-tied and googly-eyed and walk face-first into trees, tripping over your own two feet as you go. Such it was for young Bubby around Clementine.

So, I said to Clementine, "Darling, what's on your mind?"

Clementine knelt beside me and watered the potato skins I'd just planted in the ground. She said, "Pop-pop," which is what she used to call me—not to be confused with our donkey Clip-clop, of course, although I must admit I've done some dumb-headed things in my time that caused people to call me a donkey.

"Pop-pop, I've been taking stock like you said, and I figured out a couple of things that're important to me and what I truly want out of this life."

"Pray tell, daughter!"

"I want to host a Bible school right here in this mining camp."

"Clem, that's a noble goal you have, and I couldn't be prouder of you. But you realize, don't you, that you and Bubby here are the only school-aged children in the camp?"

Clem nodded her head and shuffled her feet in the dirt. "I do, Pop-pop. Which brings me to the other thing I really want to do."

"Pray tell, dear daughter!"

"I'm feeling called to go down there in the valley where the Indians live and ask their children if they'd like to come to my school."

As a father, the thought of my darling daughter embarking on a mission of this sort unsettled me something fierce. She was such a young thing—a delicate thing—that it seemed she was biting off more than she could chew.

Despite my reservations, I felt the Lord speaking to my heart. If the Lord called upon her, who was I to forbid? Could anyone of us do anything without strength from the Lord? And if I, as her earthly father, sought to keep her safe, how much more so her heavenly Father?

"Clem, if God is calling you to start a Bible school to teach the Indian children about our Lord and Savior Jesus Christ, who am I to stand in your way?"

"Thank you, Pop-pop."

"But my blessing comes with one condition. Bubby boy, here, must accompany you into the valley. Can you handle that, Bubby?"

Young Bubby bobbed his head up and down like it was tied to a line hooking a river trout. "Yes sir, yes sir! I'll follow Clem to the ends of the earth, if need be!"

"I know you will. 'Tis why I asked. Now, you two put feet to your faith and get yourselves some students!"

Well, to say 'twas a hard thing for me to watch Clem and Bubby march into the valley is an understatement; in fact, sometimes I think it took more courage to give my blessing than it did for them to go themselves. For you see, Clem had a single-minded purpose to go down there, and Bubby, well, Bubby was just like that trout on a string, but I was placing all the faith I had in God to keep a watchful eye on my daughter, my only daughter, Clementine.

I sat there beside the garden, the smell of my feet wafting in the air, watching the hillside for Clem and Bubby to return from their mission. And day turned into evening, and evening into night, until the stars pierced through the sky like a thousand cut and polished diamonds. But strangely enough, I felt no fear. God granted me a comfort in my heart that transcended all understanding, so that I slept as carefree as a baby beside the garden that night.

When I awoke to the first rays of light, birdsong filling the air, I did hear the snapping of twigs on the hillside below, and opened my eyes to a sight I could not rightly believe: Clem and Bubby leading what must have been a hundred men, women and children up the steps of our dried-out sluice, many of them carrying baskets on their heads filled with corn and squash and the greenest green beans you ever saw! Why, the harvest was bountiful enough to tide over the whole camp until the San Francisco merchants returned.

We rejoiced that night. We gave thanks to God in heaven above for his mercy! And Clem shared the gospel with the children of our neighbors, witnessing every last one of them come to a saving knowledge of Jesus Christ. In fact, 'twas the first time that any of the Indians were called Christians in that valley. Yes, indeed!

Now, getting down to brass tacks, the moral of this story, the very crux of it, is that when we set our minds to doing what is right, Jesus Himself will blaze a trail ahead of us. Or, as the Good Book puts it, in Hebrews 11:1, *"Faith is the invisible substance to which all future things owe their existence."* And there is no greater truth, dear children, that us 49ers learned that summer of 1851 than what I shared with you here today.

Trust in God, lean not on your own understanding, and have faith that He who began a good work in you is faithful and just to see it through to completion.

"In marvel of this secret, knowing that no other soul had heard those words, my heart was all aflutter—palpitating something fierce, just about jumping out of my chest like so."

The year 1865 is most remembered for the assassination of President Abraham Lincoln on Good Friday by one John Wilkes Booth, and the attempted decapitation of the United States government by his co-conspirators who planned to kill, on the very same day, Vice President Johnson and Secretary of State Seward, too. But those of us in the western territories wouldn't learn of those events for many days—no! We didn't have fancy technologies at every bend in the wagon trail to alert us instantaneously to these things. The best we had was a string of wires known as the telegraph that chirped out a series of long and short beeps in place of letters—called dots and dashes—but those contraptions were mighty rare in our parts.

Now, by happenstance, the second most important event of 1865 also transpired on Good Friday, which is the day we mark for remembrance of the saving sacrifice of Jesus on the cross. To fully understand the remarkable events that Easter weekend, we must return to the day before Good Friday, which was just regular old Thursday.

At the time, I was working for a mining company owned by an heir to the John Jacob Astor fortune, and 'twas on that day in the mining camp that at long last we shored up a shaft we'd dynamited into the side of a mountain some months before. Several of us were clearing out the deeper recesses of the tunnel, laying detonator wire and dynamite charges so we could make a second blast even deeper into the rock, when a Chinese 49er by the name Xi Li—who, incidentally, was called Tea Leaves by the other prospectors; for one, because none of us spoke Chinese, and for two, because old Tea Leaves was fond of sipping a hot cup of tea for breakfast, another one at lunch, yet a third with his dinner, and when he was feeling especially rambunctious, why, he'd even slurp down one just before bedtime. Yea, he was that kind of tea drinker!

So, all the way down at the end of that tunnel, Tea Leaves was loading up great big shards of rock and shovels full of dirt into a rail barrow—which is just like a wheel barrow except it's got a steel wheel on it so you can push it along a track, like your own little freight train—and I wasn't paying much mind to him toiling away, so what strange thing happened next only God knows for sure. But one second I could make out the rough edges of his legs and shoulders in the weak light of his whale oil lantern, and then I blinked and the man and his rail barrow was gone! They just flat out disappeared!

Now, there was only one exit to that mine. For Tea Leaves to've taken that route would've required him to back the rest of us miners all the way out of the mountain, into the fresh air and the light of day, because it was a tunnel only wide enough for a single man and his trusty barrow to pass. But had he done that? No! And that's the bitter knowledge that turned my stomach, for the only other direction Tea Leaves could've gone was down!

Oh, children, I ran faster than I'd ever run in my entire life to the end of the tunnel where Tea Leaves's lantern still swung from a support beam. And do you know what I found? Twasn't the end of the tunnel no more! Seems an unstable patch of earth had given way beneath Tea Leaves's feet, casting him into a vast cavern below. I could hear him moaning and groaning down there in the darkness—a sound, dear children, pray never fills your tender ears.

Now, fortunately for Tea Leaves, he wore a rope tied around his waist for safety that stretched all the way back up into the tunnel, so me and the other miners mustered our strength and hoisted him out of the pit. Unfortunately for Tea Leaves, he'd suffered a terrible blow to the side of his head in that fall, and we all understood the Lord was fixing to call him home.

But he wasn't quite dead yet, and this is where the story gets mighty interesting. For that's when Tea Leaves, drifting in and out of consciousness, leaned in close to my ear, and with shallow, hurried breaths, whispered, "There be great wealth in that mine—a rock like no other!"

I cradled his head in the crook of my arm and poured a little water from my canteen onto his dried and cracking lips. I asked, "A gold nugget? Is it the mother lode?"

"Not gold. 'Tis the eye of the diamond, like none you ever seen." A coughing fit overcame the prospector, ending with him spitting blood onto the rocks. Then, summoning the last of his energy, he said, "Find her, Cody—she lives!"

And with those words, dear children, he breathed his last, his whole body falling slack in my arms.

In marvel of this secret, knowing no other soul had heard those words, my heart was all aflutter—palpitating something fierce, just about jumping out of my chest like so. In fact, were anyone to have witnessed it they'd've thought a prairie dog was up inside my shirt, trying to somersault his way out! And then, a cold sweat broke out along my forehead, flowing down along my brow and mustache and beard and then coalescing into big fat drops that burst like jumping jacks when they hit the dusty ground. Yes, indeed, children—it was that kind of secret!

Now, it might be helpful for me to point out that in days gone by, when the Spanish missionaries first branched out into the lands of California, they built missions in the various places they went. This burgeoning mining town was no different. If you don't know what a mission is, why, just think of it as a church. And while I couldn't vouch if Tea Leaves had been saved by the blood of Christ, by confessing his sins and acknowledging that Jesus died for him on that old rugged cross (for I'd shared the Gospel with him, fruitlessly, on many occasions, but one should never underestimate the patience and power of God), it seemed good to me to arrange a proper Christian burial for him, seeing how he comforted me all those years before when Clementine passed.

As we carried Tea Leaves in a pine box up the worn and dusty trail to the mission, to the hillside where they buried the dead, my every thought was steeped in the secret of his diamond. Could the eye of the diamond be real? Or was the dying man delirious with fever when he whispered those words in my ear? I'm ashamed to say, children—mighty ashamed— my mind was so infused with visions of the treasure I hardly remember the funeral at all. Nay, just the dull thuds of dirt, at the end, they shoveled on the box as I hurried away.

Thoughts of that diamond took control of me, for I remember as the sun set down, I began scheming how I might get inside the mine during the night and lay hands on the rock. For you see, children, that rock represented to me something that could provide wisdom, great length of life, and wealth beyond all my wildest imaginations! But in truth, it was pure and simple greed.

After everyone fell sound asleep that night, I lay wide awake on my bedding beneath the great expanse of the heavens, gazing up at them stars all a-twinkling like diamonds. Yea, diamonds! They seemed to be everywhere I turned, reminding me of Tea Leaves's dying words, goading me back to the mine.

I reckon it was round about three o'clock in the morning when I could stand the goading no more, and so I gathered up a few supplies just as quietly as I could and skulked out of camp towards the mine shaft. My plan, you see, was to grab a lantern and a rope ladder from the supply shack just outside the mine, then make my way down that dark and lonely tunnel to the cavern that took Tea Leaves's life, and find the Rock-like-no-other he'd witnessed down there, that precious jewel that had made such a profound impression upon him just before he gave up the ghost. And that's exactly what I did!

Finding such a thing, you might think, would be an easy chore, as simple as setting my feet on the cavern floor and laying hands to that rock—assuming it wasn't too big to carry, that is. But suppose it was too big to carry? Suppose the Rock-like-no-other was the size of a pumpkin? Or a horse? Or what if Tea Leaves had seen from his vantage in the cavern that the entire core of the earth was made of one big glittering diamond? Well, seeing these thoughts crossed my mind, I slung a satchel over my shoulder and carried a hand-held pick to break off as much as I could be burdened to haul to the surface.

But after making my way through the mine shaft and descending the rope ladder to the cavern floor, I didn't see the rock that Tea Leaves had seen. Why, I saw plenty of ore lying around, and a pile of rubble as high as a man that came down with Tea Leaves in his fall, but no diamonds. And as I swung the lantern this way and that, no telltale glints of light sparkled back at me.

It occurred to me in that moment that perhaps the diamond had, in fact, originated from above, rather than below. Suppose Tea Leaves saw a glint on the tunnel floor and began digging and digging at it, until he finally reached the rock that shimmered as if it were alive, only to realize too late he had dug so deep as to undermine his very feet, causing him to plunge to the cavern floor? And the more I thought about it, the more I reckoned that was the solution—the diamond got buried in the collapse! And so, I too began to dig and dig and dig and dig!

The Great Mine Explosion of 1865

Well, children, when a person's mind becomes fixated on something, he often loses track of time, which is what happened to me that Good Friday morn. What seemed like twenty or thirty minutes digging for the diamond was in fact more than six hours, so I had no earthly clue that other people were hard at work in the mine, too.

That is, until I heard movement in the tunnel above, and somebody shouted, "All clear!"

Oh, in that moment, I realized I'd been so obsessed by the quest for Tea Leaves's treasure, that I'd made a terrible and consequential error—yea, one that threatened to end my very life! For you see, in my greed and covetousness over the diamond, I'd forgotten about my labors the day before; forgotten about laying detonator wires and dynamite charges to blast the tunnel; forgotten that Good Friday morning was the hour the mining company planned to dynamite the tunnel!

And as cruel fate would have it, the instant I set to open my mouth to cry out for help, why, a brilliant spark glinted in the pile of rock in which I'd dug all night. Yea, I spied the Rock-like-no-other! It wasn't the size of a horse, or a pumpkin even, but more about the size of a hearty breakfast biscuit. Yet, if you're schooled in the least about the value of diamonds, why, you'll understand such a stone could enable a man to live like the son of a king the rest of his days!

As soon as I laid eyes on it, I hesitated not to reach into the pile of rocks and grab hold of it. Believe you me, the way the stone fit in my hand, why, I swore it was formed in the depths of the earth for that very purpose, to be held tightly in my grasp. Most curious about this rock, though, was its astonishing weight, rivaling that of a bucket of ore! No matter, my excitement generated a rush of strength, so that with the stone in one hand and my lantern and rock pick in the other, I rose to make my way up the rope ladder, letting out a great whoop and holler—a cry of help to anyone who had ears to hear.

A voice called back, "Help!" So, I cried out again, "I'm down here!" And the voice called back to me, "I'm down here!" Oh, dear children, horror filled my heart when I heard that voice—horror to realize 'twas but an echo of my own cry to an empty mine, a mine fixing to be blasted to smithereens at any given second.

No sooner had I given my dire circumstances consideration than the TNT detonated in all its brisance, bringing the mountain down in a turbulent slide of rubble upon my head! Why, it felt like someone banged a couple of cast iron skillets on my eardrums, stuffed me in a barrel filled with mud and tossed me over a waterfall at the same time! There was no doubt—no doubt in my mind—that I'd died and passed on to my reward, because everything went black as pitch.

I can't say for certain how long I lay unconscious under the belly of the mountain, but eventually I came to— my throat dry and burning, parched and yearning for a drink of water to slake my mighty thirst. Why, I couldn't muster so much as a grunt or a groan it was so dry! All my bones ached, too, and the weight of the mountain upon me made it next to impossible to draw a single breath.

My circumstances were bleak—yea, so bleak that for the second time I wondered if I was as dead as old Tea Leaves buried on the mission hillside. But then I wiggled my toes a little—and it gave me hope. I felt the cold steel of the rock pick in one hand and the diamond in the clutches of the other, and I realized I wasn't quite dead yet!

Indeed, though yet I lived, I knew it would take a miracle to save me from this predicament. I knew how Jonah must have felt in the belly of that great fish and I cursed the rocks, despising every one of them that poked and pressed and pinned me to the ground. I wondered how God could forsake me in this time of need, and the ridiculous thought came to mind.... Oh, why won't this mountain just vomit me out of its belly? But a mountain isn't an animal or aquatic creature with a digestive system—no! It's an inanimate object which means it don't do or think anything. Even so, I began to feel a certain kinship to the rock, for it seemed to have quite a bit to teach me. After all, the rock wasn't complaining none, it was just content to be where it was at as part of the wondrous creation of God. And then there was me, feeling sorry for myself, all on account of my greed for the other rock—yea, I do mean that biscuit-sized diamond!

But the longer I lay there in the cold darkness, which stretched on for days—hungry, thirsty, not knowing whether I'd ever see the light of day again—the less significance the diamond held for me. You see, even though the flesh of my fingers desperately clung to the rock, my spirit inside turned and clung to a Rock of far greater value—yea, The Rock of Ages, Who is the resurrected Jesus Christ.

Strange as it may sound to you—for it sounds strange even to me, to hear the words formed on my own tongue—I kept repeating a single verse of Scripture over and over in my head, one I'd learned as a young lad way back in Sunday school. Do you know what the verse was? 'Twas Luke 19:40, where Jesus Himself said, *"If those who follow Me should go silent, the very rocks of the ground shall sing praises to My name!"*

And that's when it occurred to me that while my throat was too dry to cry out for help, the rocks might sing on my behalf. So, with the precious little strength I had left, I tapped the pick I held on the nearest rock in a series of dots and dashes—just like they did it on the telegraph machines I told you about earlier—that spelled out S.O.S., which is a well-known distress signal. And because of the acoustics of the cavern, the sound carried all the way up the tunnel to the other miners, who mounted a speedy rescue party to dig me out of what was nearly my grave.

When they finally brought me to the surface, why, it was Easter morning, properly known as Resurrection Day. It was a glorious day indeed! For God assured me, beyond the shadow of a doubt, He did not forsake me, despite my sinful greed; indeed, He sent His Son to die on account of that sin.

So, getting down to brass tacks, the moral of this story, the very crux of it, is that God is *gracious, merciful, slow to anger and kind beyond all our wildest imaginations!*" And that bit of wisdom, as you may know, and I'm certain you do because you'ns are sharp as whips, comes straight from the Good Book itself, Jonah 4:2 to be precise.

Now, you might've noticed I named this journal entry The Great Mine Explosion of 1865, and you probably think 'tis because there was a great explosion in a mine! But as my life stretches on and I have time to reflect on the event, the more it seems to me it ought to be called The Great Explosion of the *Mine* of 1865, for 'twas in the crucible of that great calamity I surrendered all I held as mine and reckoned it as His. Yea, that is to say, my life belonged entirely to the Lord.

If you don't yet comprehend what that means, give it time. Reflect on it during the sunups and sundowns you've got left in this world, and I'm certain it'll come to you, just as surely as it came to me.

15 TREASURE OF THE RED-HAIRED GIANTS (1866)

"He said I'd gone mad, simply seawater-drinking crazy, to believe we'd ever escape with our lives if we did such a thing."

I n the spring of 1866, the year following the death of old Tea Leaves and my near similar fate beneath the dynamited mountain which had concealed the Rock-like-no-other, I made my way to the California shipping town of San Pedro, lured by the rumor that a brash young sea captain was forming an expedition to uncover lost treasure from King Solomon's mines hidden in the Channel Islands!

Now, children, stories of lost treasure are as cheap and numerous as cornsilk suits worn by scarecrows on the plains of Iowa. But the reason I put credence in this story and abandoned a lucrative panning river on the slopes of the Sierra Nevada mountains, was because of the gentleman who first brought it to my attention. Yea, 'twas none other than Jacob Waltz, Sr, the father of none other than Jacob "Bubby" Waltz, Jr.

Old Jacob Waltz told me of a seafaring young man by the name of Jonah Bartamaeus, whose father was a wealthy California landowner. Seems the young man stood to inherit the lion's share of his father's estate, if only he earned a business degree from an Ivy League university. Trouble was, Jonah Bartamaeus preferred strong drink, swashbuckling and sailing the open seas to the teetotalling lecture halls of Princeton.

As such, he quit the university—his inheritance in doubt—determined to make a name for himself by recovering the greatest lost treasures the world had ever known. For you see, even though Jonah dropped out of school, the young captain was not uneducated by any means—no! In fact, he was known as more of a scholar than a sailor, revered for his rare knowledge of cartography, astronomy, and his abiding fascination in treasure-seeking of every kind.

The rumor that came to me that spring of 1866 was that Captain Jonah Bartamaeus had obtained an ancient treasure map from the Tongva Indian tribe native to San Pedro. This map appeared to pinpoint a vast repository of gold on Santa Catalina Island guarded by a savage, warfaring race of red-haired giants!

While tales of giants might be enough to scare off most clearheaded men, such was not the case with Captain

Bartamaeus. For you see, the Tongva Indians described a treasure of a most special sort—yea, one stolen thousands of years before from the mines of King Solomon himself. What's more, they swore whoever possessed the gold would be long of life, a guest of honor in the courts of kings, and wealthy beyond all his wildest imaginations!

You can understand how the great reward offset the great risk we'd face in due time.

Now, Jacob Waltz became entwined with the schemes of Captain Bartamaeus more by happenstance than any special kinship. For you see, Jacob Waltz was a Godly and upright man whose character ran perpendicular to the young Bartamaeus, so the fact that the two fell in league with one another might surprise some.

Old Jacob Waltz, however, left the Sierra Nevada mining camps years before with a handsome fortune of gold. He invested it in land with mining rights, reckoning that if only one of his properties contained gold, why, he'd stand to become one of the wealthiest men west of the Mississippi. As Providence saw fit, that's nearly what happened when a great earthquake altered the course of the Kern River and uncovered vast deposits of gold on his acreage up near Bakersfield.

Always looking for the next venture, he parlayed his fortune into land between San Pedro and a sleepy little pueblo to the north named Los Angeles, not so much for the gold prospecting as for the value he saw in connecting the two towns. You see, he had this notion that a railroad delivering freight inland from the seaport would pay dividends for years to come.

The elder Bartamaeus bought into this vision, snapping up Jacob Waltz' land at a premium. All of which is to say, round about the time Jonah Bartamaeus came into possession of the Tongva Indian treasure map, old Jacob Waltz was sitting on a sizable fortune, just burning a hole in the pocket of his overalls.

Jonah Bartamaeus, fearing someone might catch on about the Catalina treasure, resolved to sail at once for the island. Problem was, he had no crew and scant money since dropping out of Princeton. So, knowing of Jacob Waltz' great wealth and respecting him as a Godly and upright man—not given to double-crossing anyone—Jonah enlisted his financial backing with an agreement to split the treasure fifty-fifty, straight down the middle, once they recovered it.

I must clarify at this point that Jacob Waltz, while quite a wealthy business man at this juncture in his life, had also matured into a generous philanthropist. That's a fancy way of saying he aimed to use his wealth to help those less fortunate than himself. When he learned from Captain Bartamaeus about the treasure of the red-haired giants, why, he recognized an opportunity to parlay his fortune into far greater riches than gold—yea, he resolved to spread the Gospel to the red-haired giants as well! He agreed to fund the expedition so long as the crew included a team of missionaries.

Begrudgingly, the Captain agreed to the terms of the agreement, under condition the missionaries wouldn't interfere none with his treasure-seeking.

It was about this time I arrived in San Pedro, eager to put out to sea in search of my fortune, longing for the scent of the ocean in my nose and the song of the gully in my ear. For you see, dear children, I hadn't boarded a ship since the disastrous episode down under when I about near lost my life in that tempest on the Tasman Sea!

So, old Jacob Waltz introduced me to Captain Bartamaeus, who looked upon me with a good deal of skepticism. He needed seaworthy men, he told Jacob, not gold-panning landlubbers. Jacob pointed out, however, that Jonah knew not whether the treasure lay buried under the earth or ensconced in a cave. It stood to reason that a miner possessing his own tools—and a reputation for old-fashioned back-breaking labor—was an invaluable asset. This mollified him to some degree, but upon discovering I sailed with Captain Harry Humdinger's crew on his final, fateful voyage to the bottom of the Gulf, why, the Captain treated me as a guest of honor in the quest for the Catalina gold.

Jacob Waltz hired on the rest of the crew, along with missionaries, by the end of the following day. So it was, we found ourselves sailing out of port in Captain Bartamaeus' ship, known as the *Fairhaven*, under a favorable wind for Santa Catalina Island on Good Friday, of all days. The timing of the voyage, and the quiet of the sea, gave me time to reflect on the fact that only one year before, I'd been buried beneath a mountain, clinging to a biscuit-sized diamond.

Twasn't long, however, before the winds changed direction, and a squall blew up from the south—not dangerous, by any means—but causing us to sail further west than we were wont to do to avoid the foul weather. The maneuver would delay our arrival at Santa Catalina until late the following morning, the Captain told us; but the delay, he added with a good deal of excitement in his voice, would work in our favor.

We set anchor in a small bay on the north shore of the island, along an isthmus, taking dinghies from there to the shore. The treasure map, you see, suggested we were right close indeed to the glorious riches we all sought to lay our hands upon!

Jack Dublin

But if our expedition seems to've gone too smoothly up to this point, why, let me assure you that our good fortune was on the cusp of unmitigated disaster! For you see, no sooner had we beached the dinghies and set off on foot than a horde of the red-haired giants sprang from behind a sagebrush covered hill side, growling like wild animals and wielding spears the size of trees in their six-fingered hands. Among their ranks were nine, ten and yea, even eleven footers! We truly felt as grasshoppers in their sight.

The missionaries stepped forward first, attempting to establish a dialog with them, but all the grunting and growling made them somewhat difficult to understand. To say we were shaking in our shoes and knocking at the knees don't begin to describe our distress; and yet, for all our terror, Captain Jonah Bartamaeus stood surprisingly tall and sure of himself.

He called out to them, "Savages, we have come for the gold which you stole from King Solomon. We are not happy about that, and we want it back—on the double!"

To say Captain Jonah could not have given a less elegant speech is putting the reality of the situation mildly. Indeed, the giants worked themselves into a frenzy at this point, pulling out big clumps of their fiery red hair and even cutting themselves with their spears!

After several minutes, one of the eleven footers had calmed himself enough to step forward and string together a few words. He said, "Leave at once, or we will eat all of you for dinner!" which I suppose was even less elegant than what the Captain had said, but I wasn't about to criticize him for his lack of poetry at this point.

Captain Jonah Bartamaeus did not flinch or bat a single eyelash. He removed a watch from his vest pocket, nodded, and said the most remarkable thing I'd ever heard a man in his right mind utter, causing all of us to check the wax in our ears, not believing what he'd said. What he said was, "You will surrender the treasure to us immediately, or I will blot out the sun from sky. You have three minutes to comply with my orders."

At this, several of the giants pulled out so much of their hair they were as bald as babies. But not the cute little babies that go goo-goo-gaga and you hold in your arms—no! I do mean the giant, wild kind of babies that would crush you if you held 'em in your arms. But even as I thought this, the surrounding light began to fade. As I looked heavenward, presuming a cloud to be passing overhead, I saw only the clear cerulean sky darkening to a rivery blue and the sun seeming to be eaten away from the sky. Yes, indeed, even some of the brighter stars a man sees in the night sky peeked out of the veil!

The red-haired giants waxed terror-stricken and, sensing terrible forces combining against them, they dug barehanded and helter-skelter at the sagebrush covered hillside, exposing a veritable mountain of gold!

They cried out, "Take it, it is yours, only spare us our lives!"

The missionaries, being educated men, shook their heads in shame for the trickery of Captain Jonah Bartamaeus. The chief among them said, "See that you do not double-cross and plunder these men so."

But the Captain said, "I will now restore the sun to the sky!"

Even as he said this, the world brightened once more, and the sun appeared whole as it was before. He ordered his hired hands to load the dinghies with gold and row for the *Fairhaven*. The missionaries and Jacob Waltz, however, refused to leave, settling down on the beach to comfort the blubbering red-haired giants.

Now I, dear children, being less educated than the missionaries or the Captain, didn't have a clue what was taking place, other than I was a hired man ordered to do my job. So I did it. Then again, maybe I was just a coward. But once onboard the ship, sailing from the island, I approached the Captain who was holding a large bar of gold.

He could hardly restrain his laughter. "Those fools may be big, but they don't know astronomy. Had they known there'd be a solar eclipse today, why, we'd never've gotten off the island with our lives. Instead, they thought I held sway over the sun!"

I felt the same shame the missionaries had felt. For you see, my conscience was troubled, and so I urged him, there on the deck of the ship, to tack back around to the island and return his ill-gotten gain to the giants.

He said I'd gone mad, simply seawater-drinking crazy, to believe we'd ever escape with our lives if we did such a thing.

But I told him we ought to give it the old rah-rah college-try to ease our troubled consciences. He insisted his conscience weren't troubled in the least. I insisted it was, but he just didn't know it. Well, we went back and forth like this for the better part of half an hour until finally, at wit's end, he threatened to throw me in the holding cell below deck, and if I didn't keep my trap shut after that, why, he'd throw me overboard into the yawning, unforgiving mouth of the Pacific Ocean.

Fortunately for me, Providence did intervene, as a tempest blew up upon the sea, swelling the waves and tossing us to and fro to the point the Captain was forced to lower the sails. We took on water, and it was all I could do to bail the seawater from the ship with my trusty bucket. But it was no use—the elements prevailed!

And the Captain realized too late that for all his mastery of astronomy, no man was master of the sea. Facing certain destruction, Captain Jonah Bartamaeus ordered the lowering of the dinghies, and we managed to escape with our lives but little else as the ship capsized into the sea.

Now, tragedy in life has different effects on different people—some for good, some for worse. In the case of Jonah Bartamaeus, why, the sinking of the *Fairhaven* and its hull full of gold treasure had a humbling effect on the man.

As our dinghies washed up on the shore of Catalina Island, the missionaries and giants greeted us. Jonah was the first to disembark, falling prostrate before them, stretching out the one gold bar he salvaged from the ship.

"I've done a great evil to you and the Lord has repaid me!"

The giants, however, gathered around him, lifting him up from the sand. The chief among them, whose name was Betelgeuse, explained that while we were at sea, the missionaries shared that this was a time known as resurrection weekend, and the knowledge of Christ changed their perspective on the gold they hoarded and defended by warfare for generations. Now, they said, it was time to make better use of it.

The giants led us to the interior of the island where a vast cave concealed a hundred times the riches we'd glimpsed under the hillside. This, they said, should be shared with the world. Yea, they desired Captain Bartamaeus spread it far and wide, to bless the poor in all nations, and to share the saving knowledge of Christ as he went.

Jonah cried tears of joy, his heart transformed in the light of Christ, knowing that to whom much had been forgiven, much ought to be given back. In the years to come, Captain Jonah Bartamaeus sailed the world far and wide, feeding the poor in faraway lands, greeting kings and emperors and sultans in every corner of the globe, sharing much wealth. But I do not speak only of the wealth of gold, children—nay, but the far greater riches that come from Christ Jesus alone.

As for that old legend of the Tongva Indians concerning the treasure of the red-haired giants, did it make Jonah Bartamaeus long of life? Well, he received a reprieve from certain death on the open sea when he chose to possess the gold rather than let it possess him.

And did the treasure of the red-haired giants make him a guest of honor in the courts of kings? Indeed—but not for the sake of being known by them, but rather to make known the King of kings!

And did the treasure of the red-haired giants make Jonah Bartamaeus wealthy beyond all his wildest imaginations? Well, children, the good Captain would be the first to tell you that carrying on the work of the Lord, doing whatever it is you love best, is a wealth that cannot be weighed upon any mercantile scales.

So, getting down to brass tacks, the moral of this story, the very crux of it, is that believing what Jesus did for us should change how we use our talents. Or, as the Good Book tells it, in Ephesians 2:8, *"By grace ye are saved through faith; and that not of yourselves—it is the gift of God."*

So it was in the case of Captain Jonah Bartamaeus, was it not?

16 THE PEARLY GALLEON OF THE SALTON DUNES (1870)

"But even as I sharpened the scope's focus on the galleon, I was gobsmacked by a sight just beyond, one which I would not've believed had I not seen it with my own eyes."

Dear children, we've shared considerable time together recounting my many remarkable—yea, at times unbelievable, yet true!—experiences, expeditions and exploits, from scorching deserts to shimmering oceans, from peaks of fiery volcanoes to the *depthiest* depths of the seas. But in all my reminiscing, scouring the farthest recesses of my childhood until the present day, I am hard pressed to find a tale of stranger circumstances than the one I am about to share with you today.

For you see, back in the early summer of 1870, after pulling up stakes from the Golden Chariot mine in Julian, California (weren't no gold to be had there, only a handful of flakes I suspect was sifted on the river banks by an unscrupulous land prospector) I had in mind to follow a couple of old treasure maps in my possession that identified a sealed-up cavern in the Grand Canyon. The maps described a cache of Dynastic Egyptian artifacts—yea, even sarcophaguses of pure gold, and perhaps something greater!

'Twas during the early stages of this endeavor, as my faithful donkey Clip-clop and I made our way east from Julian toward the Salton valley, which lies due north of the Gulf of California and a smidgen southwest of the Mojave Desert, that we settled down for the night in a small oasis town a thousand miles from the nearest sea.

I tied off Clip-clop's reins at the communal trough where he guzzled the cold artesian well water for better than a quarter hour. I slaked my own thirst at the well-pump for about as long, before giving old Clip-clop a thorough rub down with a boar's hair brush and rinsing the dust from my eyebrows, mustache and beard. As we reclined at the trough, relishing in our rehydration, a strong breeze and swirling sand cloud blew in from the desert. And here's where the story gets mighty strange, children, for out of the midst of that cloud emerged three spectral figures—yea, like the figures of ghosts—skeleton-thin, shoeless, and covered in blisters, bandages and ragged clothes. I rubbed my eyes forwards, backwards and sideways—thrice—before convincing myself they were real.

As they staggered towards us, Clip-clop brayed uncertainly. The first figure appeared no better than a blind man with bandages sealing off his eyes, grasping at the air before him; the second figure resembled a mummy with bandages crisscrossing his head, wrapping his ears and rendering him deaf to the whirring wind; and the third one wore a belt slung under his chin and cinched atop his sunburnt, balding head. I made haste pumping water into a pail, then hurried to meet the hapless trio on the wagon trail.

"Friends, you look like dead men walking. Get some water in you before you'ns give up the ghost!"

The three men obliged, gulping from the pail. Each swallow resounded in the night like the emptying of a deep glass jug until at last the pail was drained. To my relief, the men looked a hair's breadth less close to death than they had mere moments before.

I led them off the wagon trail where they released the weight from their sand-calloused feet and rested against the splintered wooden trough just as if it were as comfortable as a goose down mattress. All I had to offer the men in the way of food was a few filets of salted herring meat and some hardened crusts of bread, but they treated it as the first-fruits of quail and manna, which brought a measure of radiance to their cheeks. For the first time since laying eyes on them, I suspected they just might survive their ordeal.

It was at this point the man with the bandaged eyes offered me introductions, saying his name was Charley. Then, reaching out to feel the bandaged ears of the man beside him, he said, "This here is Marley. Poor fella—can't hear so much as the sound of his own beating heart no more. The other one is Harley."

Harley nodded, slowing churning his jaw, but only managed to eke out a guttural response that sounded something like, "*Brum-brum-brum-brum-brum-brum.*"

Clip-clop brayed at this, pinching back on his hooves as far as the slack in the reins allowed.

Charley explained they had set out from the oasis three days earlier with a group of treasure-seekers, pursuing what the local Indians described as an old Spanish galleon—that is, a masted, ocean-going ship—stranded in the shifting desert sands and laden with a hull full of priceless black pearls!

Only once they located it, the other treasure-seekers, scoundrels that they were, double-crossed them, putting out Charley's eyes the way the Philistines did to Samson in days of old; they boxed Marley's ears with such force as to burst the eardrums therein, rendering him to deaf to the world; and to poor Harley, why they reached inside his mouth and gave his tongue such a fierce twisting that he hadn't spoken an intelligible word since, just that *brum-brum-brum-brum-brum* sound that spooked the wits out of Clip-clop.

Now, before you go and say that such a tale, of a Spanish galleon half-buried in the desert sands a thousand miles from the nearest sea, is all balderdash, I should point out that in my travels throughout parts of Mexico and South America, in my dealings and trading with the Indians of those parts, I came upon no less than three maps which depicted California as an island!

For you see, dear children, as the Indians tell it, from time to time, earthquakes rumbled the earth in such ways as to lift or lower parts of the earth, changing the courses of mighty rivers so that they flowed and emptied into low-lying areas that previously stood dry. In fact, they speak of a time when a ferocious earthquake along the San Andreas fault did alter the courses of the Colorado and the Sacramento Rivers, sinking the mouth of San Francisco Bay so that the ocean rushed inland. The resulting deluge formed a vast, navigable sea from the Gulf of California to the Klamath mountains. In fact, the Indians set traps along the shores and hauled in mollusks to their hearts' content!

So, when old Charley spoke of a pearl-laden Spanish galleon in the Salton dunes, I did not think such a thing was entirely far-fetched. And what's more, when Charley reached into the pocket of this tattered pants and removed a black pearl the size of an olive, I knew the Spanish galleon of which he spoke was no desert mirage.

Now, one would think that after the great torment and disfigurement that Charley, Marley and Harley had suffered at the hands of the double-crossing treasure-seekers, a return trip to the Spanish galleon would be the last adventure on their minds. But you'd be wrong! Yea, Charley explained that the chest of pearls had been too much for the treasure-seekers to spirit away with their supplies on hand, consisting only of a wheel barrow and a couple of mules (both of which were ill-equipped to ford the Salton dunes) and so they set out in search of reinforcements.

Even though they took his eyes and Marley's ears, and even though they took Harley's voice—who Charley said could sing like a finch on an April morn before the wrenching of his tongue—the last thing he desired to see was those wretches laying hold of the Spanish galleon's bounty for some nefarious end. As such, he entreated me and my fearless companion Clip-clop to follow them into the desert to retrieve the chest of black pearls from the hull of the galleon.

Now, dear children, if you know the first thing about me by now, it ought to be that I'm always up for a good adventure, especially one where there be treasure involved. Furthermore, I'm not one to back down in the face of seemingly impossible odds. No! Indeed, 'tis how I became the richly blessed man I am today!

And so, after taking our fill of sleep under the starry oasis sky, we arose the next morning just as the first rays of sunlight set the horizon aglow. Charley reasoned that since the eye-, ear- and tongue-snatching scoundrels had not turned up at the oasis overnight, they must have sojourned east toward the town of Ehrenberg, where supplies were more plentiful, so they could regroup before making another go at the Spanish galleon.

That regrouping afforded us a small window of time in which to gather what few supplies were on hand at the general store—namely, a few shovels, a good heavy rope for hoisting out the chest of pearls and several sticks of dynamite for blowing the hull, if need be—and formulate a plan of our own.

In retrospect, however, the plan we devised was fuzzy at best, and downright dangerous to any clear-headed individual. But we were all a little soupy in the brains on our three-day journey toward the galleon. Yea, the trek was fraught with searing temperatures, too little water and countless missteps retracing Charley's path.

Charley said he was following the wind at his face, which had been at his back on the hike out, but the wind had changed directions.

When I wrote with a stick in the sand for Marley, asking why he didn't lead us, he said he didn't remember the way, since they had followed Charley out. And when I asked Harley why he didn't lead us, he said, "*Brum-brum-brum-brum-brum-brum.*"

Oh, it was a fruitless endeavor, one that might well have cost us our lives were it not for Charley's heightened sense of hearing. For you see, at that precise moment, when all seemed lost, Charley stopped in his tracks, shouting, "There, listen! The sound of the galleon's sails!"

The rest of us heard not of which Charley spoke, so I reached into Clip-clop's saddle bag and pulled out my looking scope. Lo-and-behold—there, in the distance, half-buried in the sand, stood just about the most beautiful sight I had ever seen—the Spanish galleon! But even as I sharpened the scope's focus on the ship, I was gobsmacked by a sight just beyond, one which I would not've believed had I not seen it with my own eyes. Yea, several miles beyond, following an ancient, dry riverbed that snaked away from the Colorado River, was a second ship, all sails raised, appearing to sail the desert floor just as true as if she were on the high seas. I tightened the focus of the scope, observing wheels mounted to the hull of the ship, only to hear Charley say, "Oh no—that laugh. That hideous laugh!"

I shifted up the scope and spied a tattered flag bearing a crest of two interlocking letters—'C' and 'G'—flapping high atop the mast of the wheeled desert sailship. When I trained the scope on the captain at the helm, a terrible knot seized my innards, for I beheld a ruddy, baby-faced man with a twisted smile not even a mother could love. It was none other than *L'Enfant Terrible*, Crysco Gringo! We made haste for the pearly galleon and reached her before that wicked bandit, but with the wind at his back, Crysco bore down on us at a terrific rate of speed.

Charley said, "I hear his sails now. If Clip-clop rode with all the fury in his hooves, could the two of you reach the Colorado River before Crysco reaches us?"

But I needn't answer, for Clip-clop reared up on his hind legs and brayed the finest bray of any donkey in his generation.

Charley said, "You have to blow a hole in the side of the Colorado River and flood this entire valley. Me and Marley and Harley will sail the galleon onto glory. Now go! Godspeed!"

I leapt on to Clip-clop, who churned through desert sands like a mighty locomotive, determined to undermine whatever fiendish plans the baby-faced bandit sought to unleash with the wealth of the chest of pearls. So it was, we reached the banks of the Colorado before Crysco reached the galleon, and laid dynamite to the rock walling up the river from the valley below.

When it blew, why, the roar was of a thousand battle cannons, and the slide of rocks like the felling of a great mountain.

The roiling waves of water overtook Crysco's sailship, dashing it to the valley floor, then continued on to the galleon where I prayed those waves would slow and gently lift her from the grip of the dunes. But, as difficult as the truth was to face, I think I knew in the deepest mineshaft of my heart that those waters would not slow. I think old Charley, Marley and Harley knew it, too. As those waters surged ahead, I consoled myself with the knowledge that those three brave treasure-seekers gave up all those pearls—yea, even their very lives—so that Crysco Gringo should not prevail, but that I should live.

That show of self-sacrifice, dear children, taught me the truest meaning of love, reminding me of Another; the One who paid it all, that as many as who believed in Him should not perish, but have eternal life.

So, getting down to brass tacks, the moral of this story, the very crux of it, is that you should love your neighbor as yourself, just as Charley, Marley and Harley did us. Or, as the Good Book puts it in 1 John 4:10, *"Herein is love, not that we loved God, but that He loved us, and sent His Son to be the propitiation for our sins."* Now, if that word *propitiation* confounds you, dear children, fret not—it's just an Ivy League way of saying He gave His life to pay for our sins. And pray tell!—what in the world is easier to understand than that?

17 THE ASTOR MIDAS MACHINE, PT.1 (1870)

"As we descended the fraying rope, torches in hand—knowing the jagged mouth of the mine shaft would at any moment bite the line in two— the cavern below suddenly yawned with light. I beheld a river of pure quicksilver, flowing in two directions, and beyond it, the warbling gears of an unworldly mechanism, throwing off sparks and threatening to fail."

Looking back on my long and extraordinary life, the summer of 1870 represented a crossroads that challenged me beyond what I dared to dream, and tempered me, like a newly forged blade plunged in the river rapids, beyond any strength I expected of myself. For you see, dear children, after departing the Salton Dunes, where Charley, Marley, and Harley met their noble ends to prevent *L'Enfant Terrible* from laying cruel hands upon the Spanish galleon filled with black pearls, Clip-clop and I unfolded a couple of old treasure maps and set off, once again, for the perilous clime of the Grand Canyon—which is another way of saying the days were blazing hot, food was scarce, and we had no right to expect we'd live to see another full moon. No! 'Tis a fact, as we traveled east, sensing the worst lay ahead of us, that I penned my Last Will and Testament. Clip-clop would have done the same, no doubt, but held off on account he lacked brains, possessions and opposable thumbs with which to hold a quill!

One of the treasure maps we followed related to the rumored existence of a sealed-up cavern in the Grand Canyon said to contain ancient Egyptian artifacts—yea, even sarcophaguses of pure gold! If you don't know what sarcophaguses are, why, those are the coffins you find mummies in!

How such artifacts came to be in the canyon was a mystery to the original owner of the map, causing him, in time, to doubt the credibility of the legend and conclude it was all an elaborate hoax. I, on the other hand, recalled in sharp relief my encounter in the canyon, years before, with the dreaded Songstress of old, that winged and horned, riddle-spitting Sphinx. At the time, I chose not to pursue the treasure guarded by the beastly statue, pursuing instead a treasure of far greater worth—that is, my brotherly friendship with White Feather and his tribe.

But the reason I was itching to get back to the Grand Canyon related to the second treasure map in my possession, one which I drew with my own hand based upon clues I'd gathered over the years. In fact, the main reason I purchased the first map pertaining to the Egyptian artifacts was because upon seeing it, it did so neatly mirror my own hand-drawn map! That said, one notable difference existed between the two. You see, children, the canyon map I bought told of golden sarcophaguses, but the map I'd drawn suggested some kind of King Midas machine existed in the canyon capable of extracting gold from the magma of the earth's core! Yea, according to the maps, the two treasures resided on the same piece of earth!

But for you to fully understand the remarkable, life-altering tale I am about to tell, it is first necessary for you'ns to learn the untold history of how the California Gold Rush of 1849 began. Most of you, being the bright children you are, are well-steeped in the facts regarding the discovery of gold at Sutter's Mill on January 24th, 1848. What you don't know, however, is that the owner of Sutter's Mill, one John Sutter, was in debt to money lenders the world over, not the least of whom was that famed New York fur trapper, the wealthiest man in America, John Jacob Astor.

Now, a curious series of events occurred over a span of 66 days following the discovery of gold at Sutter's Mill that would prove to alter the course of American history—yea, of the entire world! For you see, dear children, Sutter's Mill was in the California Territory of Mexico, and in January of 1848, why, the United States and Mexico were entangled in a raging war, the outcome of which was far from certain. And yet, a mere nine days after the discovery of gold at Sutter's Mill, the nation of Mexico inexplicably signed the Treaty of Guadalupe Hidalgo with the United States to end the war. Even more inexplicably, Mexico agreed to sell 525,000 square miles of their nation to the United States for a sum of 15 million dollars! Now, to be fair, 15 million dollars was a great deal of money at the time; but considering the vast deposits of silver and gold subsequently discovered beneath those desert sands, why, the sale price of 15 million dollars might as well have been 15 cents!

More curious still, 'twas rumored that John Jacob Astor brokered the war-ending treaty, gifting the United States Treasury the 15 million dollars necessary to buy the Mexican territories. Since Astor was lending money to both the United States and Mexico for the war effort, why, he possessed considerable leverage at the negotiating table. Yea, it is said that, in addition to the pile of cash shelled out, he forgave Mexico their entire war debt!

The question I'm sure you children are asking yourselves is why would Mexico accept such a deal on Astor's terms? The forgiveness of that hefty war debt comes to mind. But what did Mr. Astor stand to gain? Curious question, indeed! Perhaps the answer is as simple as this: the treaty allowed Astor free access across the land to mine for gold. But a more curious wrinkle in this tale, which cannot be neglected, is that eight weeks to the day after ratification of the treaty, John Jacob Astor died.

Even though Mr. Astor was a socialite, patron of the arts, and the wealthiest man in America, he was buried in a private ceremony to little fanfare in a Manhattan churchyard. His grave marker stands to this day—not a cross, or a headstone, as some of you may reckon, but rather a tall, white obelisk with the words 'Astor Vault' embossed on the side. If you're wondering what in the world an obelisk is, why, it's an object the same shape as the Washington Monument in our nation's capital.

Now, before your eyes go all droopy on me, as I see some of them are, I assure you there is an important reason for retelling all this history to you'ns. Yea, lean in close that you do not miss it! For you see, an obelisk has its origins in ancient Egypt, so it stands to reason that any man who would choose an obelisk to mark his grave was pointing his finger back to that civilization. Considering that Astor was a patron of the arts, who trafficked in Egyptian artifacts for New York museums, why, you can see how the Canyon Sphinx, my treasure map and John Jacob Astor's intervention in the Mexican-American war, seemed not coincidental in the least. Nay!

Now, this part of the story may shock the daylights out of your tender souls, but I have it on good authority that eight weeks to the day after the signing of the war-ending treaty, John Jacob Astor didn't die at all. No! The facts I have pieced together suggest he faked his own death, for the nefarious purposes I am about to reveal.

In the early days of the 49er Gold Rush, which actually began in 1848, when word first leaked about John Sutter's gold discovery at the mill, neophyte prospectors—which is another way of saying they were inexperienced gold diggers—fanned across the newly annexed American territories in search of their fortunes. Many a man staked his claim on a promising tract of land, only to find abandoned mine shafts where solid rock ought to be. 'Twere as if someone had stripped the countryside of gold, silver, and copper long ago. But who could have mined the land? Well, that, dear children, is the greatest mystery never told! As much as I'd like to tell you the story around this campfire, I must save it for another day.

For now, the important point to fix in your minds is that I purposed to follow through to the end my search for the canyon treasure. Now, you may recall from a prior journal entry that way back in the early years of the Gold Rush, after Clementine and I made a hasty retreat from Angel's Mining Camp, that we found ourselves in the Grand Canyon, where we forged a lifelong friendship with Chief White Feather and his tribe. So, once I purposed to decipher the treasure maps in my possession, why, it made perfect sense to seek out White Feather for his aid in the matter. I figured no living man would have more to say about the maps than Chief White Feather.

But instead of hiking straight to Chief White Feather, I took a circuitous route—which is to say, I took a longer route—for the express purpose of tracking down a man I knew to be living in the canyon at the time. I reckoned his knowledge of the canyon would be invaluable on my quest. That man was none other than Jacob Waltz, Jr, better known to you'ns as Bubby. Seems after his old man struck it rich on land deals in California, Bubby followed the call of his heart which was to establish a business along the Colorado River to guide travelers to safety (although I suspected he was a-searching for those 500 silver eggs!)

Bubby, at one time in his life, feared the water something fierce, seeing that he couldn't swim to save his life, nor that of my darling daughter Clementine. Now, don't get me wrong—I am not laying blame at the feet of Bubby for the girl's untimely demise—I'm simply pointing out that the tragedy had a very definite effect upon the young man, whereby he determined to defeat his fear of water by conquering the rapids of the Colorado River. And that's exactly what he did!

Clip-clop and I arrived at Bubby's base camp to find him reclined upon the gravel beside a campfire, roasting a skewered snake for dinner. But upon seeing us, he dropped the serpent into the fire, showing utter disregard for the hunger in his belly, that he might fall into my arms and greet me as his own father. Yea, had Clem lived, I've no doubt that, in time, the two lovebirds would have married.

Bubby clung to me for a considerable span of time, shedding tears on my shoulder and begging my forgiveness for the tragedy long ago. You see, Bubby had penned me a letter of condolences, years before, that summed up his belief that I blamed him for her death. Nothing could be further from the truth! Even so, we held each other for the span of a quarter hour, comforting each other for one we loved who was lost and gone forever.

That evening, I showed Bubby the maps, but he concluded they must be hoaxes, given certain inconsistencies contained therein. For starters, he pointed out the obvious that they both referenced different treasures. But, he also noted that the central feature of the maps—a large mountain beyond the horseshoe bend in the Colorado River—did not exist. Nevertheless, Bubby said he was not the man best-suited to address the matter, but that we should consult Chief White Feather.

The next morning, we made haste to White Feather's camp, where the old man greeted us like long lost family. He grieved with me for Clementine's passing, saying he first heard of it by way of a campfire song that had grown in popularity in the canyon (which, incidentally, Bubby himself had penned.) We partook of baked beans, cornbread and roasted squash as we caught up on the comings and goings of nearly twenty years, before I reached in Clip-clop's saddlebag and unfurled the maps before White Feather.

The Chief examined them, nodding as he traced his finger along the maps, muttering unintelligible words. Then, he rolled up the maps and handed them back. "Our prophets said this day would come."

"Your prophets? What in tarnation are you speaking of, White Feather?"

"The man who sold you the map had no faith."

Bubby squirmed where he sat, biting his tongue, but to no avail. "Pardon me, Chief White Feather, but 'tis a hard thing for a man to have faith in a mountain that does not exist!"

"You mean to say, a mountain he cannot see."

"Forgive the boy." I put a hand on each man's shoulder. "What he means to say is, the maps agree, and yet they don't make a lick of sense! What does that have to do with faith?"

"The maps are perfect in what they describe." White Feather stood, pointing a long, boney finger to the horseshoe bend in the distance. "Do you not see the mountain?"

Bubby and I leaped to our feet, shielding our eyes from the sun, suspecting we'd missed something on the horizon. But 'twas as before, no mountain to be seen. I said, "Help our unbelief!"

Chief White Feather narrowed his brows. "The reason the man who sold you this map thought it was of no value is because he did not have eyes to see. If he did, he would have understood the map points not to a mountain above the canyon, but beneath it. Come, I will show you the way."

To say those words lit a fire under me and Bubby and Clip-clop would be an understatement! Yea, they ignited a conflagration 'neath us akin to the Great Great Plains fire of 1824! And so, we set out into the canyon in search of our fortunes, no matter that we could see a storm brewing in the distance. But it was not a rainstorm. Nay, 'twas the dread haboob—which is a thick dust storm no different from a wall of sand blowing every which way.

Perhaps it would've been better had we heeded the approaching storm, for it soon enveloped us like a great boa constrictor, squeezing us on all sides, until Clip-clop, blinded by the driving sand, staggered off the trail into a ravine below. We only located him because of the faint bray of the beleaguered beast.

Oh, dear children, to say Clip-clop got himself into a terrible pickle wouldn't be stating the half of it, for upon close inspection, White Feather determined that Clip-clop had fractured his foreleg. Us three men dragged the donkey into a nearby cave, set the bone, fashioned a splint, and poured a measure of water into a divot in the rocks from which he might slake his thirst. Then, undaunted by the haboob, we set out to locate the entrance to the underground mountain.

As we pressed on toward our goal, White Feather explained that the ancient, abandoned mine shafts of which we'd heard were not drilled by his ancestors—nay, nor by the Conquistadors—but existed as far back as the Indians recorded their history in the stars. While most shafts were picked clean of any worthwhile ore, and dead-ended in the depths of the earth, one shaft continued to that fabled mountain we sought. It was at that shaft that White Feather stopped, removing tumbleweeds set there to disguise the entrance.

"We will use ropes from here on, for the decent is long and treacherous." White Feather stood solemnly still, allowing us a moment to gather our wits, to continue or abandon our quest.

Looking to Bubby, he nodded his head. I nodded back, let fly into the shaft the coil of line slung over my shoulder, tying the daylight end of the rope to a rock outcropping. I led the way into darkness, with White Feather on my heels and Bubby pulling up the rear.

The tunnel was sterile and smooth, the walls neither possessing nor requiring any shoring of timber, for they appeared to've been carved by a great circular drill that fused the rock in place as it cut. After descending a hundred yards, however, the grade of the shaft steepened, requiring us to light torches, plant our boots on the rock and hang on for dear life! And after another hundred yards, repelling with my back to the unknown, my feet slipped out into thin air, and I dropped like lead, using only a single bare hand and the soles of my boots on the rope to arrest my fall, causing not a few friction-burns in the process. When at last I ceased falling, I swung to and fro like a clock pendulum nearing the final hour. 'Twas all I could do to hang on with my blistered and bloodied hand while not letting go the torch!

The distant calls of White Feather and Bubby echoed by me in waves. I waved my torch in signal before feeling their weight accumulate with mine on the dangling line. Then, I heard a ping and a whiz and we dropped several feet, which I took for a bad omen. It seemed the rope was being chewed apart where it rubbed on the rock above. Oh, dear children, if you've experienced this yourselves, you can agree it is a frightening circumstance indeed! But what were we to do, other than descend the tattered line in hopes the cavern floor arrived at the end of a carful descent, rather than at the end of the opposite kind?

And so it was, as we descended the fraying rope, torches in hand—knowing the jagged mouth of the mine shaft would at any moment bite the line in two—the cavern below suddenly yawned with light. I beheld a river of pure quicksilver, flowing in two directions, and beyond it, the warbling gears of an unworldly mechanism, throwing off sparks and threatening to fail.

I could make out the ground below (which gave me blessed hope!) and a vast cavern filled with Egyptian hieroglyphs, totems, gold trinkets, and sealed vases containing what God only knew. Truth be told, I struggled to keep pace with the fantasies my imagination dreamt up! Yea, as my feet touched solid earth, I beheld a towering obelisk, whose peak stabbed into the darkness above and whose base stood at the shore of the quicksilver stream. On the opposite shore, Astor's King Midas machine churned full force.

The cavern smelled—strange as it sounds—like the coming of a thunderstorm and radiated a withering heat. The gears of the machine ground against one another, spinning inside and whirling about on unseen axels, with all the power and heft of a hundred locomotives. Every few moments, the machine seemed to catch, loosing an eardrum-splitting screech, spitting off white-hot gear teeth that splashed in the quicksilver to hisses and puffs of smoke.

In the midst of the gears loomed a golden disk engraved with the figures of animals and people, wobbling like a top losing its spin, about to tip on its side. It appeared strangely familiar to me, though I couldn't quite place my finger on it. But the longer I examined the figures—a lion, a coyote, a scorpion, a man with a water jug—it became clear to me I was not seeing mere pictures, but a depiction of the heavenly constellations. Where the brightest stars in those constellations would be, magnificent jewels adorned the disk! However, one of the jewels had gone missing—the one at the throat of the coyote—perhaps shaken loose by an earthquake or faulty workmanship.

White Feather and Bubby set down in the shadow of the obelisk, gazing in wide wonder at what we had found. Then, Bubby pulled off his hat, letting out a whoop and holler. "He did it! Old man Astor faked his death!"

White Feather stretched out his arms as if to silence Bubby and prevent us from going further. Even so, he stepped out of the shadow of the obelisk, moving toward the river, to view the machine in all its magnificence. "Mr. Astor did not build it. When my ancestors arrived in the canyon at the end of the ice age, the machine was already here, slaving under its own power."

I joined White Feather on the quicksilver shore. Standing so near to it, I felt an electric charge lift the hairs of my mustache and beard. And with my eyes now adjusted to the meager light, the sheer, angled walls of the cavern that tapered upward—toward the peak of the obelisk—took shape, and I realized we stood on the inside of a gargantuan pyramid. Yea, 'twas the underground mountain White Feather promised! I said, "But if John Jacob Astor didn't build the Midas machine, pray tell, who did?"

"It's not a Midas machine." White Feather gazed into the gears with a look of dread and awe on his face. "It is the engine of the world, and it is breaking down."

The quicksilver river began to froth—great bubbles expanding and bursting from some unimaginable pressure beneath—until red-hot magma gurgled up, mixing with the mercury and sinking back below.

Suddenly, I understood the design of the machine was just as my map predicted: as the gears turned, it pulled magma filled with liquid gold to the surface, mixing with the quicksilver like an enormous sluice. And the jewels set in the disk served as ballast—which is a fancy way of saying they balanced the wheel. The missing weight of the jewel, then, was causing the machine to fail.

I pointed it out to White Feather. "If we reset that jewel, this contraption should run smooth as glass."

But White Feather shook his head. "The legends speak of a king who came here long ago, from across the ocean. He claimed the Eye of the Diamond as his own."

Now, dear children, I could hardly believe my ears! The legends of White Feather's tribe, when considered alongside my encounter with the Canyon Sphinx, the coyote of Hangtown, and the Rock-like-no-other, fit together like the strakes of a watertight ship. I blurted out:

"Rameses!"

The blood drained out of White Feather's face and his chin quivered in the torchlight. "How did you know the king's name?"

"It ain't important!" I grabbed hold of the rope dangling in the darkness and hoisted myself up. "But what's of utmost importance is getting back to Clip-clop. What are you two waiting for? The engine of the world is breaking down!" And off I climbed into the darkness, ascending with the speed and nimbleness of a spider on its web.

My decision to return to the cave at that moment marked the crossroads of the summer of 1870 of which I spoke earlier. Events followed which I can hardly find words to describe, nor would you be likely to believe them if I did!

And so, it seems only proper that I delay the sharing of those things until your tender minds mature to fathom them.

So, getting down to brass tacks, the moral of this story, the very crux of it, is that if you ever face an obstacle the size of a mountain, remember that God created mountains to be climbed. Or, as we like to say in the mining camp, *"God skillfully shaped us before time began for such a time as this."*

Knowing that the Creator of all has laid such a charge upon our shoulders, who among us will idle by while the promise of the future awaits?

To that end, dear children, seek ye God, find your purpose, and up the adventure!

ABOUT THE AUTHOR

Jack Dublin grew up in New England, West Germany, and Virginia; and is a graduate of The University of Arizona. He lives in parts unknown with his beloved bride, their four darling children, and a fancy bearded dragon.

A NOTE FROM THE AUTHOR

Reviews are gold to authors! If you enjoyed this adventure, will you consider rating and reviewing it on Amazon or Goodreads?

OTHER BOOKS BY JACK DUBLIN

—◆—

The Lost and Found Journal of a Miner 49er: Vol. 2

The Lost and Found Journal of a Miner 49er: Vol. 3
(Spring 2019)

JOIN THE RUSH

—◆—

The adventures of the Miner 49er continue in *The Lost and Found Journal* series by Jack Dublin. Want to find out what happens next? *The Lost and Found Journal of a Miner 49er: Vol. 2* is available now, and *Vol. 3* releases in Spring of 2019. Sign up for Jack's mailing list to be the first to know when it comes out!

Join the rush at https://jackdublin.net/free-download.html

HI-FIDELITY ADVENTURES

Listen to *The Lost and Found Journal* series on audiobook, performed in glorious hi-fidelity by Jack Dublin. Scan the QR codes below with your smart device to sample Volumes 1 & 2!

The Lost and Found Journal of a Miner 49er: Vol. 1

The Lost and Found Journal of a Miner 49er: Vol. 2

FOLLOW JACK ONLINE

@TheJackDublin

#UpTheAdventure